A SMALL SLAIN BODY

M. Pinaud, the celebrated detective of the *Sûreté*, is sent to the seaside resort of Rouplage to investigate a brutal kidnapping and murder. The local jeweller had been found dead just outside the town. He had been stabbed and then run over by a heavy vehicle. Beside him was the dead body of his young daughter, who had been kidnapped a few days before. As Pinaud conducts his enquiries, the complicated plot unfolds — until it reaches a completely unexpected and startling climax . . .

PIERRE AUDEMARS

A SMALL
SLAIN BODY

Complete and Unabridged

LINFORD
Leicester

First published in Great Britain in 1985 by
Robert Hale Limited
London

First Linford Edition
published 2004
by arrangement with
Robert Hale Limited
London

British Library CIP Data

Audemars, Pierre
    A small slain body.—Large print ed.—
Linford mystery library
    1. Murder—France—Fiction
    2. Kidnapping—France—Fiction
    3. Police—France—Fiction
    4. Detective and mystery stories
    5. Large type books
    I. Title
    823.9'12 [F]

    ISBN 1–84395–155–X

Published by
F. A. Thorpe (Publishing)
Anstey, Leicestershire

Set by Words & Graphics Ltd.
Anstey, Leicestershire
Printed and bound in Great Britain by
T. J. International Ltd., Padstow, Cornwall

This book is printed on acid-free paper

To Joan,
for her love,
her courage
and her kindness
while it was written

The small slain body,
the flower like face
Can I remember if thou forget?

A.C. Swinburne

Itylus

Prologue

In the days when M. Pinaud had retired to his old house in an obscure country village he derived a great if perhaps childish satisfaction from laying his log fire in the immense mediaeval stone fireplace.

Each autumn and winter morning he would carry into the front room a bucket for the ashes, an old dustpan and brush and the wood he had sawn and chopped in the summer months from his beautifully stacked and immaculate woodshed.

There in the fireplace, beneath the shadow of the great cross beam, the ashes would be shovelled and the hearth swept. Then two large rectangular billets of wood, split from a sawn section of trunk, were placed carefully parallel, lengthwise, on edge. A few small flat sections, sawn all exactly to the same size from an old plank, were then laid across to support the handfuls of kindling, small dried

1

branches and twigs that he added.

Five or six fairly thin logs were stacked upright on the outside of each of the two billets and two or three more laid carefully across the kindling.

There were, naturally enough, variations on this theme, according to the supply of wood, but the principle always remained the same.

Then, in the late afternoon or evening, once all his unending tasks had been completed, he would strike a match, light and insert the pumice-stone firelighter, which had been soaking in a jar of paraffin the whole day, between the two parallel billets of wood, pull up the armchair, and watch the leaping and roaring flames with a grunt of satisfaction. In a few moments the whole mass of wood was ablaze. Then, with careful discrimination, he could begin to add the heavier logs.

There were always pictures to be seen in the fire. Without switching on the light they seemed more vivid and real. In spite of the hundreds of times he had laid this fire, always more or less in the same way, they were invariably different. He stared at them and watched them with affection and remembered the past . . .

★   ★   ★

It was there that his chronicler found him, dreaming of other days in front of his fire.

The bottles and the glasses were swiftly produced from the cupboard. M. Pinaud lifted a massive log and fed the brightly burning fire.

'How nice to see you once again,' he said with great sincerity. He approved wholeheartedly of this earnest and dedicated type, who had spent a lifetime in recounting some of his more celebrated exploits in book form.

'And you too — looking so well,' replied his chronicler, addressing his remark to the small table at which M. Pinaud was busily dispensing large and generous drinks.

'And what a beautiful new suit,' added M. Pinaud over his shoulder.

'Yes,' agreed his chronicler, stroking

one sleeve of the rich and impeccably cut material complacently with his forefinger. 'I just had it made.'

'But why wear it to drive a car into the heart of the country? You might have had a puncture.'

The reply was unexpected.

'It was Handel, was it not, who always put on his best suit whenever he sat down to compose?'

M. Pinaud suddenly poured wine on to the tablecloth as well as in the glass. He knew that Germaine his wife would castigate him severely, since they had now so few good tablecloths left. He kept his back turned while he felt for a handkerchief to wipe the moisture which that charming compliment had brought so easily and so quickly to his eyes. After all, what were a few old tablecloths compared to precious moments such as these?

He turned and held out a brimming glass.

'That is a very nice thing to hear,' he said quietly.

'Thank you. And what have you been doing with yourself since I last saw you?'

'Oh — nothing very much,' M. Pinaud replied, bringing his own glass to the fireplace and resuming his seat in the armchair by the fire. 'Mainly chopping and sawing wood for the winter. Half of the great ash tree in the churchyard was split in the recent gale and Father Palissier was only too pleased when I offered to pay to have it sawn down and brought here. The Church owns so many *hectares* of forest land around here that he is never short of wood.

'What with that, cutting the lawns for the last time before the winter, weeding the flower-beds, picking and storing the apples, repairing the sheds and the garage, which are all falling to pieces, cleaning out the gutters once the house-martins have gone and the drains after the leaves have fallen, making bonfires of the rubbish — there has not been a great deal of time to spare.

'You know, my friend,' he continued thoughtfully, sipping his drink with a great and noble satisfaction, 'a great amount of cock has been uttered about the happy state of retirement — how then at last a man has time to do all the things he has secretly longed to do throughout his working life — to do them in his own time and in his own way, without interruption or interference from other people.

'This is not true. This is the cock I mentioned. There just is no time. I have never worked harder in my life — only trying to accomplish the tasks necessary to live in the country.'

He drained his glass in one long and ecstatic swallow, levered himself out of the armchair, and stood waiting patiently, one hand outstretched, until his chronicler felt in honour bound to emulate him. Then he went to the small table and busied himself with the bottles.

'From the impressive number of duties you have just enumerated,' his chronicler replied politely, 'and knowing too well myself that there are only twenty-four hours in a day, I am bound to agree with you.'

'Good,' said M. Pinaud heartily, pausing reluctantly in his pouring when it became evident that neither glass could hold any more.

'But what you have told me is really a very good thing.'

'Why is that — '

'Because I have known several immensely rich men, who had worked extremely hard all their lives, so that they could make enough money to retire early and find time for what they really wanted to do. They had everything — beautiful old houses and gardens in the country, cars for every occasion, motor-boats and sailing yachts, television sets, holidays abroad — everything you can think of. And in a year or two they were dead.'

'Why?'

'Sheer boredom, I should think. Nothing or not enough to do — after slaving for most of their lives to retire in peace and comfort.'

There was a short pause while M. Pinaud reflected.

'Maybe you have a point there,' he said at last.

'Yes. I know I have. But on the other hand,' his chronicler continued, with all the implacable determination of one who knew that he held the best cards in his hand, 'in your case it is different. You have got to be reasonable. It is no good looking modest and pretending that you have retired. Some people — more now than ever before — definitely enjoy reading about you and your exploits. Think of the American royalties in your last cheque. And they already want another book. That is why I came here. What about the kidnapping of M. le Chef's niece?'

M. Pinaud resumed his seat by the fire. He contemplated the pile of logs in the corner, selected one with careful deliberation and placed it on the fire. He drank deeply and then spoke slowly and musingly as he remembered.

'But that was the one case I did nothing to solve. That was not a case but a nightmare. There was no case. There was no proof. There were no clues. I searched the cottage myself and found nothing to — '

'But you found out the truth,' his chronicler interrupted quietly.

'Yes. And I have been trying to forget it ever since.'

'But how many parents should be grateful to you? He would have gone on — he would have kidnapped others — had it not been for you.'

M. Pinaud did not answer.

In the flames of his own log fire he could see once again those other flames as the petrol tank exploded like a bursting flower with nightmare petals. And he could only watch because he was on the top of the cliff and the other car had plunged over the edge into the sea below and the exploding flower became at once a blazing torch which the dark surging waves quickly extinguished.

He was no longer sitting at ease in an armchair watching his own fire. He was sitting once again, tense and rigid, in the driving-seat of a car on the edge of the headland, looking down at what had once been two men in a blazing taxi — and now was nothing but a cold grey waste of heaving water.

And he knew that he would always remember. He knew that he could never forget, because that was his very nature.

Then he remembered the small dead

body of the jeweller Mansard's daughter in the morgue at Rouplage. In his vividly intense imagination he pictured what must have happened to the others — to those who had not died but only disappeared, and he shivered suddenly in front of the blazing flames.

His decision had been the only one. He knew that he had been right. He had no regrets. He had done his duty as he had seen it, for the sake of the other parents, as his chronicler had expressed it.

*   *   *

With an effort he roused himself from his day-dreaming, stood up and busied himself with the bottles.

There could be no question of objecting to his chronicler's suggestion. After all, he owed this man a very great debt, and he always did his best to pay his debts and honour his obligations. One passed through this life but once — there was no time to pay them all. This intelligent character had spent so many years in writing about him and his exploits — it would be unworthy of their friendship to refuse.

His sudden smile transfigured the hard brooding lines of those strong features that had seen a lifetime of so much pain, cruelty, injustice and violence.

'Of course,' he said quietly. 'I am sorry.'

They spent a very happy evening together discussing the new book, until the great pile of logs in the fireplace had diminished to two or three, and there were considerably more bottles on the carpet than on the table.

They talked on and on, and neither of them even heard the mellow chimes of the English fusee and chain bracket clock on the sideboard.

M. Pinaud mentioned the spare bed-room, which Germaine always kept ready, and was glad when his offer was accepted. He now had a legitimate excuse to get more logs from the woodshed and more bottles from the cellar, so that this forthcoming and outstanding book could have all the attention it so richly deserved . . .

And as he busied himself with these

tasks, which because of their dear familiarity occupied only a small part of his mind and attention, he continued to think about Handel. His chronicler's thought had been an eminently noble one, and to him completely acceptable. After all, there were very few who had ever composed anything as beautiful as the Largo.

1

It all began on a beautiful summer's morning when M. Pinaud had been peremptorily summoned to that dignified and austere office on the first floor in the *Quai d'Orsay.*

M. le Chef looked up from the only chair in the room and smiled across his desk with what was for him an unusual benevolence and charm.

M. Pinaud stood formally to attention. After all, this old bastard, in spite of his trying ways, did pay the salary which had enabled him to enjoy the love and companionship of his wife and family. His innate sense of proportion would not allow him to do otherwise.

Some of his fellow detectives, he had heard, whose exploits had never even reached the other side of the Atlantic, slouched and lounged and boasted. One had actually tried to sit on the corner of the desk. He was no longer employed by the *Sûreté*.

'Ah — yes, Pinaud.'

'You sent for me, m'sieu?'

'I did. If I am correct, you are not engaged in anything of vital importance at the moment?'

'No, m'sieu.'

'Your wife and family are away on holiday?'

'Yes m'sieu. To the farm of her parents in Morillon.'

'And you told me that you had one or two things to do at home, and that therefore you intended joining them later?'

'That is correct, m'sieu.'

'Well, I am very sorry, Pinaud, but you will have to put that off. Rouplage is the other way on the coast.'

'Rouplage, m'sieu?'

'Yes, Pinaud. That is where you are going.'

He reached for a sheet of blank notepaper, studied it carefully, and then continued.

'Rouplage is a very prosperous and

popular seaside resort on the north coast, rather more than one hundred and fifty kilometres from here. You turn off the N1 just before you get to the sea. There is a signpost. It consists of one long curving promenade full of hotels and boarding-houses behind a good beach. A few moments' walk to a sandy bay with breakwaters. A small harbour, mainly for fishing-boats. On each side of which the roads climb to the cliffs. The town itself is a good way from the station. The line runs inland. A long walk with a suitcase.'

M. Pinaud wondered, not without some justification, if he were reading from an open holiday brochure on some other part of his blotting-pad. All this informa-tion could certainly not be on a single sheet of blank notepaper.

But M. le Chef had attained an emi-nent enough position to come to the point in his own time. He paused and smiled again.

'Just putting you in the picture, Pinaud,' he continued. 'Now then. To business. The local jeweller in Rouplage, by name Mansard, was found dead just outside the town yesterday morning. He had been stabbed and then run over by a heavy car or truck. Beside him the body of his young daughter. Also dead. A blow on the back of the head with something heavy, like a hammer or tyre-lever. She, apparently, had been kidnapped a few days before, and had not been seen until yesterday. According to the local Inspector at the *Préfecture*, Dumont, there are no clues.

'But as you know, that does not mean anything. There are always clues, if you look in the right places. I have only spoken to him on the telephone, but this Dumont seems to me to be something of an idiot.

'That is one reason why I would like you to go up there yourself. The other reason is a more personal one.'

He paused. M. Pinaud did not say anything. He was here to listen, not to speak. His thighs were beginning to ache, but that was something he would admit only to himself. Perhaps one day, if he worked hard enough, he too might sit in a comfortable chair behind an ornate desk and tell others what had to be done, completely regardless of how many private and personal plans might be disrupted.

'I knew Robert Mansard personally,' the quiet incisive voice continued. 'He was a good friend of mine. My own niece, Marie Lahaye, was going to stay with them for a few days' holiday. His wife died two years ago, but Marie always kept up their friendship. She was at the same school for a short time with the child, who was a good few years younger.

'All the plans had already been made. Naturally at this dreadful news they were immediately cancelled. But Marie needs a holiday, and so I booked a room at The Golden Lion there and persuaded her to have a few days' rest.

'That is why I would like you to go there yourself to-morrow. This business has shaken me badly. Go yourself. Keep an eye on her. See Inspector Dumont. He will tell you everything you need to know and show you the bodies — I have organised that too — and find out who murdered Mansard and his daughter.'

'I will do my best, m'sieu.'

'I know you will. I have told Marie to telephone you to-night at home as soon as she gets to the hotel. About eight o'clock. The train is due in at seven-thirty. I also told her to take a taxi from the station — it is a good way to the hotel. I am seeing her off myself to-night from the *Gare du Nord*. She has assured me that she will telephone.'

M. le Chef stood up and held out his hand.

'That is all, then. I am most grateful to you.'

'I shall be glad to help.'

'Good. And, Pinaud — take great care. These people — whoever they are — are playing rough.'

Before she left Germaine had cooked him an enormous Danish ham in a profusion of carrots and onions. Their second largest saucepan was filled with boiled potatoes. He could carve and either eat the ham cold, with lettuce and tomatoes, or heat it up with the vegetables and potatoes. There would be a minimum of work and waste of time and a maximum number of two of his favourite meals.

Now he lifted the lid of the saucepan and contemplated the ham gloomily. Would it keep? He had no idea how long this business at Rouplage would take him. He would almost certainly have to stay there for several days. He could not drive back one hundred and fifty kilometres each day to finish it. Should he post it to Germaine and the children? It had cost a fortune.

He sighed and went to mix himself a drink.

He found, as he had so often found before, that the contemplation of all his worries and problems through the bottom of an empty glass, or in this case several empty glasses — since the heating of the ham and the frying of the potatoes proved a lengthy task to one unaccustomed to the intricacies of cooking — undoubtedly diminished their intensity and their menace to a remarkable degree.

By the time he had replenished his large plate three times and emptied a litre bottle of wine his anxieties regarding surplus and wasted food had greatly diminished.

He sighed philosophically, stood up and lifted the lids from the saucepans. There was really not a great deal left. If he got up early he could finish most of it for breakfast.

Then he looked at his watch. It was well past eight o'clock. This niece of M. le Chef, Marie Lahaye, was supposed to have telephoned at eight o'clock. He sighed again. Women in general, in spite of their many and admirable qualities, had usually very little idea of punctuality and no sense at all of the urgency of time. And the train might have been late.

He washed up, laid the breakfast table in preparation for an early start, made a pot of coffee and went to find the bottle of brandy which his cousin Mathilde had sent him for his birthday. This he eventually located under the clean tablecloths in the sideboard drawer, hidden there cunningly but vainly by Germaine for emergencies and important guests.

He took it into the kitchen, where he could keep the coffee hot and handy, and again he looked at his watch. It was nearly nine o'clock. The train must have been very late. It was the height of the season. Many people went to the seaside.

He poured himself a cup of coffee, filled a large glass with brandy, sat down at the table and lit a cigarette.

M. le Chef would not telephone. Why should he? He could not know if the train would be late in arriving after he had seen her off. And by now he had probably gone out for the evening, or else disconnected his telephone, as was his habit, in order not to be disturbed during that intensely personal relaxation which was typical of the somewhat complicated aberrations of his sexual life. But if for any reason he had not seen his niece on the seven-thirty train, then surely he would have let him know, since it had been agreed that she would telephone.

He sipped a little more brandy and confirmed that the scalding hot black coffee ensured that it arrived at its appointed destination.

He lit another cigarette and — now that M. le Chef was in his mind

— remembered all his help in the past with nostalgic affection. At times he had proved infuriating. He had objected, obstructed, thwarted, delayed, impeded, curtailed, rejected, criticised, hampered, contradicted and even sometimes deliberately cancelled many of his own bold and constructive propositions as to the handling of certain cases — but never had he let him down.

M. Pinaud felt very strongly that he owed certain obligations to this eccentric and erratic character who was also his employer. Quite apart from these obligations, there was the duty he obviously owed to the man who paid his wages.

He finished the cup of coffee while it was still hot and drank some more brandy. Then suddenly he stood up, found the correct telephone directory under the boots and shoes in the cupboard, went to the telephone and dialled the number of The Golden Lion hotel in Rouplage.

The ringing tone ceased.

'Yah?' said an adenoidal female voice.

'Hullo. Is that The Golden Lion?' he

asked, wondering whether he had the right number. Surely the correct answer from the best hotel in Rouplage should have been delivered in a courteous and enthusiastic manner, something like — good-evening, this is The Golden Lion Hotel at your service — can I help you?

'Yah,' repeated the voice again.

'Good. Could you tell me if a Mademoiselle Marie Lahaye has booked in from Paris. She was due in Rouplage at seven-thirty.'

'Couldn't do that. No idea.'

'Well,' he replied, controlling his emotions with some difficulty, 'Would you look in the register and find out — '

'What's that?'

'What is what?'

'Register.'

'The hotel register. The book in which people sign. It should be in front of you.'

'Never seen one. We're ever so busy. I'm only standing in for my sister Clarisse. She had a discharge sudden-like. Awful pain in her guts. Asked me to keep an eye on the desk when she ran. Had it last month too when — '

'Look — get me the manager on the telephone, will you?'

'What name?'

He made a great effort and successfully eradicated any interest in sister Clarisse from his mind and thought swiftly. At this stage, and with this moronic half-wit, there was no point in announcing or introducing Pinaud of the *Sûreté*. Far better to wait and hear what the manager had to say.

'Tell him it is a personal call.'

There was a long delay. No-one replied when he spoke into the mouthpiece. The sister of Clarisse had obviously abandoned her post without another word and gone in search of the manager.

Then suddenly he heard a voice.

'Correvon here. I understand that you wished to speak to me.'

It was a bluff and hearty voice. M. Pinaud pictured him, quite erroneously, as a large, bluff and hearty type.

'Yes, thank you, M'sieu Correvon. Would you be kind enough to give me a little information about one of your guests?'

'Who are you?'

Again he thought swiftly. M. le Chef might not approve of the inhabitants of Rouplage knowing that Pinaud of the *Sûreté* was investigating what was probably a local crime — at least not until he had seen Inspector Dumont. Any hotel was a great place for rumour and gossip.

'My name is Pinaud. I am a friend of Mademoiselle Marie Lahaye, who had a room reserved at your hotel and was due to arrive tonight on the seven-thirty train from Paris. It was arranged that she would telephone me as soon as she arrived, at about eight o'clock. She has not done so. I am beginning to worry as to whether she arrived safely.'

'Just one moment, M'sieu Pinaud. I will look in the register.'

'Thank you.'

This time the delay was not long.

'Are you there, M'sieu Pinaud — you said the name was Lahaye?'

'Yes. Marie Lahaye.'

'No — there is no-one here of that name. The reservation is entered, but she has not signed in.'

'Are you quite sure? She was seen off at the *Gare du Nord* this evening, on the train that arrives at seven-thirty.'

'Just one moment. Hold on, please.'

The voice, when he heard it again, was now somewhat less bluff and not quite so hearty.

'Of course I am sure. I have the register here in my hand. She might have missed the train or — '

'That is unlikely, since she was taken to the station and seen on it.'

'She could have changed her mind here and gone to another hotel.'

'But why? You say the room had been reserved for her.'

'I have no idea. The train might have been delayed.'

'Have you got the number of the station?'

'No, I have not. And may I say that I am a very busy man, M'sieu Pinaud — this is the height of our season. Why don't you look it up yourself and find out? I am sorry I can't help you, M'sieu Pinaud. Good-bye.'

The line was disconnected. M. Pinaud

hung up. Rude bastard, he thought. M. le Chef's opinion of the best hotel in Rouplage must have been based on false information.

He went back into the kitchen. It was obviously the time for more coffee and brandy. In the firm belief that his supposition was justified, he made a fresh pot of coffee and removed the cork once more from the bottle of cousin Mathilde. And opened another packet of cigarettes.

What should he do now, he wondered. M. le Chef's niece had obviously not arrived at her hotel. M. le Chef had seen her off on her train, or else he would surely have telephoned.

He stood up and went to the telephone again. He dialled the number of M. le Chef. As he expected, he heard the engaged signal. Which meant that his respected employer was almost certainly in bed with some popsy and enjoying himself so much that he did not wish to be disturbed.

He replaced the receiver, thinking that in all fairness he should concede that there was an undeniable reason for such a precaution. A telephone bell can ring at the most awkward time — even *au moment critique* — and can serve no useful purpose at any stage of copulation.

Moodily, he went back to the kitchen table. The coffee was still beautifully hot, and cousin Mathilde had been generous enough to make her bottle a large one.

But he could not rest. He could not relax. As soon as cup and glass were empty he was back at the telephone, riffling rapidly through the pages of the directory until he found the correct number.

'S. N. C. F. Rouplage,' said a deep and pleasant masculine voice. 'Can we help you?'

He sighed with relief. A somewhat definite improvement on the sister of Clarisse and her discharge, he thought with considerable thankfulness.

'I am sure you can. Good-evening to you. Would you be kind enough to tell me whether the seven-thirty train from Paris arrived on time this evening?'

The reply was instantaneous.

'To the minute, m'sieu. As it always

does. The best train of the day.'

'Thank you for your courtesy and your efficiency. Good-bye.'

Back once more at the kitchen table he held cousin Mathilde's bottle up to the light. What was left would be of no possible use in an emergency nor of the slightest interest to any important or influential guest. He therefore emptied its contents into his glass and drank it far too quickly while he made his decision with characteristic swiftness, since the brandy was of an exceptional quality which deserved a restrained and appreciative consideration.

Then he stood up, went into the bedroom and fetched the small suitcase he always kept packed for emergencies, made a quick tour of the flat to check the windows, the taps and the lights, locked the back and front doors and made his way down the stairs to get his car from the garage.

2

Once clear of the city, he put his foot down hard on the accelerator and roared up the N1 at a speed far in excess even of his own normal standards. Which is not a statement to be lightly dismissed.

In this he was helped by circumstances. At that hour there was very little traffic on the road. In the morning there would have been cars towing trailer caravans, family cars with children and dogs in the back, lorries with and without trailers, powerful company cars with hard-eyed commercial travellers speeding to their clients in the next town, even tractors towing farm-carts to the next village, but now there was nothing — only the unwinding road streaming beneath the flow of his powerful headlights and the black poplar trees seeming to merge into one dark and continuous curtain to veil the pale moonlit sky behind.

Who but an idiot would drive one hundred and fifty kilometres to the seaside at this time of night, he asked himself moodily as he swung out without diminishing his speed to pass a courting couple contorting themselves frantically — and yet not surprisingly, considering the basic physical requirements for copulation — on the back seat of a very small saloon.

It was not until he had to slow down for a curve that he found time to answer his own question. When driving a powerful car very fast at night it is a golden rule to think only of what one is doing.

Perhaps not an idiot. But certainly a man with a conscience, a man who believes in honouring his obligations, a man whose experience of crime over the years had given him an acute sense of knowing instinctively when something was wrong — a man like you, Pinaud.

He accelerated once again as the road straightened ahead and the majestically tall poplar trees seemed to beckon him on even faster.

When he wrote to thank cousin Mathilde for her gift, perhaps he could suggest that she made it two smaller bottles instead of one large one next time. Had she done so for this birthday, he might well have left earlier.

He remembered M. le Chef's travel brochure talk, used his spotlight on the signpost, turned off the main road and eventually came down the steep headland hill into the main promenade of Rouplage.

A very polite pedestrian gave him explicit instructions, and in a few moments he had parked his car in the forecourt of The Golden Lion hotel.

★   ★   ★

Clarisse, at the reception desk and switchboard, was something quite different from her sister. Pretty, charmingly polite, and suitably clothed in a white silk blouse and black jacket and skirt, she not only looked the part but acted it efficiently.

'Is M'sieu Correvon expecting you,

M'sieu Pinaud?' she asked. 'He is a very busy man — '

He smiled.

'So he has already told me on the telephone earlier this evening. Thanks to the help of your sister, I had a few moments' conversation with him. Now I would like a few more.'

She laughed — with the happy care-free laughter of a child.

'You must be a man of considerable ability, M'sieu Pinaud — if you succeeded in doing that. It is an achievement for poor Yvonne to insert a telephone-plug into its right socket. To her, this is a devil's box. Just one moment.'

And M.Correvon, when he appeared, was also quite different from the impression given by his bluff and hearty voice. He was also very slightly and aggressively drunk, and began to sway gently until he placed a hand on the reception counter to steady himself.

'Now then — what is the meaning of all this nonsense? I did not expect to hear from you nor see you again, M'sieu Pinaud.'

He was a small man, but very powerfully built. His forehead was broad, with receding smooth hair, his eyes pouched, bulbous and dissipated. M. Pinaud looked at him and did not like him. He was careful to keep his voice expressionless as he spoke.

'If you remember, M'sieu Correvon, I asked you a question about a Mademoiselle Lahaye, who booked a room here in your hotel and has not come to claim it. I felt I was justified in expecting a certain amount of civility, courtesy, goodwill and practical help, as a potential client, from the manager of the finest hotel in Rouplage. Therefore I came here myself, so that to-morrow morning I can try to find out what has happened to her. I will take the room you are holding for her.'

To-morrow he could be Pinaud of the Sûreté and there would be no arguments. To-night he was tired after a hard day's work and an exhausting drive.

The manager had flushed at M. Pinaud's words, started to say something and then changed his mind. Perhaps the counter had started to move as well as the floor.

'If you wish,' he said indifferently. Then to the receptionist; 'Clarisse, give M'sieu Pinaud the key of the room we are holding for Mademoiselle Lahaye. You will find the number in the reservation book.'

He turned back to M. Pinaud.

'As I told you on the telephone, we are extremely busy, and I am not particularly interested in potential clients. I have quite enough money of my own. Good-night to you both.'

He pressed hard on the counter and successfully pivoted himself around in the direction of the open door through which he had come.

'Good-night, m'sieu,' said the young lady.

'Good-night,' said M. Pinaud.

With a skill no doubt engendered by countless repetitions, M. Correvon successfully and triumphantly aimed himself accurately at the open doorway, stepped over the threshold in the nick of time and slammed the door shut behind him.

M. Pinaud looked at Clarisse. But she was already turning the pages of the register. He was tired, but there was still one more thing to be done.

'Am I keeping you up, Mademoiselle?' he asked politely.

She looked up, reaching for the keyboard, and smiled.

'Oh no, M'sieu. I stay until everyone is in. There are still three more to come.'

'Good. Then would you be kind enough to give me another half-hour — I must run the car down to the station.'

'Of course.'

'Thank you. I will not be long. How do I get there?'

'Where is your car — in the forecourt?'

'Yes.'

'Turn right as you come out. Straight down the promenade. Second on the left.'

'Thank you once again. *Au revoir.*'

*   *   *

The station building was high, ornate and old-fashioned. It had been painted periodically since its construction at the end of the previous century, but not altered in any way. There were two sets of lines and two platforms, connected by an overhead iron bridge, a level-crossing barrier across the road to the town centre at one end beside the signal-box and a marshalling-yard with warehouses, engine-sheds, points and sidings at the other. The yard extended parallel and behind the far platform, the arrival one was immediately behind the facade of the building.

An extensive forecourt gave access to the station, with two small roads, one at each end, for entrance and exit. At the moment there was one taxi waiting outside the building and two private cars.

He parked his own neatly parallel and in line, got out and climbed the three steps to the entrance. The booking-hall was immediately inside. He walked across and spoke into the open louvres of the circular window.

'Good-evening to you.'

'Good-evening, m'sieu. I am afraid we are closed for the sale of tickets.'

M. Pinaud smiled. He recognised the

deep and pleasant voice immediately. This courteous elderly man with a mane of long white hair was the one who had answered his telephone call so politely and helpfully.

'That does not matter. I do not want one. Just a little information.'

'Of course, m'sieu. How can I help you?'

'Is there another train due in from Paris to-night?'

'Yes, m'sieu. The last one from the *Gare du Nord* will be here in a few moments. That remains here and leaves as the first departure to-morrow morning, as this is the end of the line. Then we close the station.'

'Do you expect many passengers?'

The man laughed and shook his head.

'You saw the forecourt as you came in, m'sieu. One taxi. To-morrow morning there will be a line of them as long as the station. Who comes to the seaside at this time of night?'

'Who, indeed. Perhaps you can help me. I will wait for this last train. I am expecting a young lady with a suitcase who should have arrived on the seven-thirty train — but did not. Were there any other trains this evening from Paris after the seven-thirty?'

'Only one, m'sieu. It came in at nine-thirty.'

'You did not notice or see — '

The man shook his head, politely and regretfully.

'I am unable to help you, m'sieu. I was busy in here all the time with tickets and the telephone. Your best plan is to have a word with the porters — the same two are still on duty until this last train gets in.'

'Thank you. I will do that. Thank you once again for your courtesy and your help. Good-night to you.'

'Good-night, m'sieu.'

★   ★   ★

The two porters were wheeling an empty luggage trolley from one end of the arrival platform to the other. This they achieved in silence and with a solemnity befitting the importance of their task.

M. Pinaud waited patiently until they

had run the trolley up against the wire mesh fence beside the signalbox and then accosted them.

'Excuse me,' he said politely, 'I know that a train is due in and that you are very busy, but could you give me a little information?'

'Of course, m'sieu,' one of them replied immediately.

'Apart from a thousand other duties, this is why we are here. This is the object of our existence.'

This was the short one, a man with a powerful thickset body, a red face, an almost bald head and a huge curved nose. He had a voice of immensely resonant power, even when speaking normally. M. Pinaud could imagine what it would be like when announcing a train's destination for the benefit of its passengers. His companion was a gigantic youth with the physique of a prizefighter and a completely vacant expression. He looked at M. Pinaud without interest and said 'Ar.'

M. Pinaud, perhaps optimistically, took this to signify that he was in complete agreement with his companion's sentiments.

'Thank you,' he said. 'On the seven-thirty from Paris this evening, can you remember if a young lady, travelling alone and carrying a suitcase, got off here?'

The short porter rubbed his nose thoughtfully with a grimy hand.

'I seem to remember someone like that,' he said slowly, 'But I just can't be sure. Too many passengers. There were quite a few on the nine-thirty to-night — but not so many as on the one before. That is the big one.'

'Ar,' confirmed his companion.

'If she did,' the man continued, ignoring the interruption, 'and if she had luggage to carry, she would undoubtedly have got into a taxi — quite a few came back for the nine-thirty, although not so many as for the seven-thirty. That is the big one. A line of them from one end of the building to the other. No-one walks with a suitcase.'

'Ar,' said his companion once again.

'What did she look like — this lady friend of yours?'

'That,' M. Pinaud replied regretfully, 'I cannot tell you until to-morrow. I have not seen her myself. I am making enquiries for a friend of mine. But to-morrow I will give you a photograph of her and a full description of what she was wearing.'

'That is sensible. Very sensible indeed. That will be a great help. Then I will be able to remember whether this one was your lady friend. What has happened to her?'

'She did not get to The Golden Lion, where she had booked a room.'

'That — that is nothing. She went to another one.'

'But this one was recommended by her uncle.'

'No matter. That does not mean a thing. What is an uncle to a young girl?'

'But he booked her a room.'

'This sort of thing happens all the time. She did not like the receptionist's face or manner. Or she might never even have gone there. She might have met someone on the train, some young bastard with an

42

oily smile, a saleman's tongue, tight jeans and only one thought in his mind. There are fifty-eight other hotels in the town to choose from. We all know what young girls are like, m'sieu.'

'Ar,' volunteered his companion, who obviously knew as well and was determined not to be excluded from the conversation.

But M. Pinaud was not satisfied. He too, knew what young girls and even women were like, but he could not imagine this particular young girl, with the upbringing she must certainly have been fortunate enough to enjoy as the niece of M. le Chef, wandering through a town at night, carrying a suitcase and looking for a hotel when her room had already been booked at the best one there. In spite of whatever blandishments, exhortations or temptations any eloquent fellow traveller might have been inspired to employ.

He opened his mouth to speak, but at that moment there was the sudden clanging of a shrill and raucous bell as the barrier came down across the road, the thunder of a diesel-electric engine and the grind of a braking train.

Both porters were galvanised automatically into action.

'Sorry, m'sieu — on duty now.'

'All right. Thank you for your help. I will see you to-morrow.'

'Ar,' said the young one as he passed.

The train whispered and glided down the length of the platform. And as he walked out past the booking-hall that astonishingly powerful voice roared out in a soaring crescendo of volume far exceeding his wildest imagination; 'Roulage — Rouplage — end of the line — Rouplage — all change for Rouplage.'

* * *

When he returned to the hotel Clarisse was still behind the counter.

'I do hope I have not kept you up — ' he began.

'Oh no, m'sieu. There is still one to come.'

She handed him a numbered key.

'On the first floor.'

'Thank you. Call at seven o'clock, please. Is there a telephone in the room?'

'Of course.'

'Good. Would you give me an outside line, please.'

Her hand reached out to the switch-board.

'That is done. Good-night, m'sieu.'

'Good-night and thank you.'

He climbed the wide staircase, walked along a corridor and opened the door. The bedroom was large and beautifully furnished, with an adjoining bathroom. The air-conditioning made it delightfully cool. He dropped his suitcase, took off his jacket and sat down at the telephone. Then he dialled the number of M. le Chef's flat.

The bell rang and continued to ring. He has gone to bed, Mr Pinaud thought moodily as he glanced at his watch. It is hardly surprising. Worn out with an evening of frenetic fornication, he is now in bed and fast asleep. Let the bell ring and go on ringing. It is bound to wake him up in the end, if I keep it ringing long enough. Other people too are tired. I have not had an easy day. But how can I go to bed until I have told him? This is important. This is something he must know.

The bell continued to ring for what seemed an interminable time. And then suddenly its tone was replaced by a loud and irate voice demanding to know who the bloody hell was the unprintable lunatic mad enough to disturb a man in the middle of the night.

'Pinaud here, m'sieu,' he replied quietly, answering the perfectly justifiable question and accepting his new status without argument.

'Pinaud — did you say Pinaud?'

'Yes, m'sieu.'

'I must be dreaming. I was fast asleep. I have been asleep for hours — '

'I am sorry, m'sieu. I tried to 'phone you before, but the line was engaged.'

Not many people dared to interrupt M. le Chef, but in this case, he thought, the circumstances had their own justification. He continued quickly with what was important, in order to forestall further recrimination.

'Did you see your niece on the train, m'sieu?'

'Of course I did. I told you I would. I am not in the habit of — '

For the second time M. Pinaud transgressed the unwritten law and interrupted. There seemed no signs of progress in this conversation, but it had to go on. He had to tell him. Then perhaps he could go to bed himself. Deliberately he spoke rapidly and concisely, allowing no time for interruption.

'I thought you did. Or else you would have 'phoned me. Your niece did not arrive at the hotel. I drove up to Rouplage this evening when she did not ring and I am staying here in her room at The Golden Lion. I have already been making enquiries at the station. One porter has a vague recollection of her arriving but is not sure. Therefore would you send me to-morrow by hand as soon as possible a photograph and a description of her clothes and suitcase. Then I will see what I can do.'

There was a silence. A very long silence. He waited patiently. When M. le

Chef eventually replied his voice had completely changed. It was soft and slow and sad. It was the voice of an old man. There were no recriminations, no reprimands, no questions and no comments.

'I will do that. Thank God you are there, Pinaud. It was good of you to drive so far — so late. And thank you for waking me up.'

'I thought that both things were what I ought to do, m'sieu.'

'Yes — but only you would have thought of doing them. Thank you once again. I will send what you need in the morning. Keep in touch. Good-bye for now.'

'Good-night, m'sieu.'

And then he went to bed.

3

In the morning, in the bright sunshine as he drove away, he saw what had not been clear in the pale glow of the street-lighting the night before — that The Golden Lion was a beautifully proportioned three-storey rectangular building, and had almost certainly been a coaching inn some several centuries ago, isolated in what was once its own garden. Traces of an ancient flint wall that had formerly enclosed it still remained on three sides of the forecourt.

The *Préfecture*, on the other hand, was a vast square of cement blocks on the far side of the town, by the harbour.

He parked his car and walked in the front door. A burly policeman, ex-Army sergeant type, looked up from his desk and switchboard.

'Yes, m'sieu?'

'Inspector Dumont, please.'

'He has just come in,' the man began

doubtfully. 'He is very busy — '

'So am I,' interrupted M. Pinaud with a smile that justified the interruption. 'He will see me. Pinaud of the *Sûreté*.'

His voice was quiet and gentle, but the policeman shot out of his chair as if someone had barked a parade-ground order.

'Just one moment, m'sieu.'

He marched across the room, knocked on and opened a door on the far side, and disappeared for exactly two minutes. At the end of that time he re-appeared, closed the door and marched back. His craggy features were now transfigured by a welcoming smile.

'This way, please, M'sieu Pinaud.'

'Thank you.'

Inspector Dumont was already standing and holding open the door of his office.

'Come in and sit down, M'sieu Pinaud,' he said. 'I was expecting you, but not so early.'

'Thank you.'

Dumont closed the door, waved to the chair in front of his desk and walked on to sit behind it. He was a tall and powerfully built individual, clad in a very expensive and beautifully tailored suit. His head was massive, with heavy jowls, a wide mouth and a high and intellectual forehead. His voice was loud, sonorous and majestic with authority.

'There is no need for me to say how pleased I am to see you, M'sieu Pinaud,' he began. 'I heard you were coming here because of this Mansard business. I am responsible for this roughly triangular coastal strip as far south as Rouen and Le Havre — of course, there they have their own offices and their own organisations. These are places of importance. The salaries are commensurate. Hence this backwater is in my jurisdiction. You come with very high authority indeed, M'sieu Pinaud. I am naturally completely at your disposal and will do my utmost to co-operate and show you whatever you wish to see.'

'Good. I understand that Mansard's daughter was recently kidnapped?'

'Yes. Five days ago. I will show you two letters I found in his desk while searching for some clue. He did not bring them to me.'

'Have you had other, similar cases here?'

'Well — yes — two or three have been reported, but I have not been able to do much about them.'

'Indeed — and why not?'

'Because after the first initial report to us here, we have had no further information or enquiries for news of our progress, which would be natural in the case of a genuine kidnapping. I therefore presumed that the missing persons turned up. If there had been an actual kidnapping and a cash ransom were demanded, most people would be able to find or borrow the money somehow. This is preferable to having the missing person harmed in any way.'

He paused for a moment and then lifted two sheets of paper from the desk and held them out to M. Pinaud.

'I think it is time I showed you the two letters I found in Mansard's desk,' he added. 'Then perhaps you will be able to understand better what I mean.'

M. Pinaud took them and read them. They were scrawled on two separate sheets of cheap notepaper in what was obviously a disguised hand. The first one was short.

We are very careful to treat our guests with every consideration at first while the money is being found. Naturally there can be no contact, only isolation, and a mask is worn when food is brought in.

If the money is not paid on demand, then we have other outlets abroad for our merchandise and the organisation to ensure that no clues are ever left. Your daughter is still young, but she has definitely reached the age of puberty.

His breath came quickly and unevenly and he saw a red mist of rage in front of his eyes. Through it he was aware of Dumont looking at him curiously, but the Inspector did not speak. Perhaps not many people have my imagination, he thought, as he read the other sheet. The second one was even shorter.

Leave fifty thousand francs in a plain sealed envelope on the exit end of the central table in the Post Office at Rouplage at eleven o'clock precisely on Saturday the fifteenth. Go straight out and walk away. You will be watched all the time. Your daughter will be returned to you at once, safe and unharmed.

He folded them over and passed them back. Dumont took them, laid them on his desk and leaned forward in his chair,

'Now you see what I am up against,' he said. 'Cheap notepaper from our local stationer — tens of packets sold every day. Cheap ball-pen. Same thing. No fingerprints — must have worn gloves.

'Mansard went about boasting that he would get her back himself. He had no faith in the police. He was one of those self-opinionated jewellers who — because they have specialised in a certain subject and can stick a glass in one eye, consult a

Mohs scale and tell you exactly what your diamond ring is worth — then because of that presume that they know something about everything. He was one of those. He would not listen to me. He knew better. Now it is too late.'

M. Pinaud sat without moving in his chair, lost in thought. He did not answer. It was Dumont who broke the silence.

'Perhaps he was speaking the truth. Perhaps he did find out something by himself. That explains why the pattern was changed and both were killed. Or perhaps it was meant to silence him and the child was killed by accident. Because in these other cases I mentioned to you, and from this letter, it would seem that once the money has been found there is no violence. That would explain why I have never heard any more beyond the first preliminary report.'

'That could be,' agreed M. Pinaud. 'Have there been any other incidents recently — apart from those you mentioned — which perhaps fall into the same category?'

'Yes. I was going to tell you. There have

been one or two young girls reported missing. But I have seen no more of these letters.'

'What did you do?'

Dumont shrugged his shoulders, a gesture as eloquent as words.

'What could I do? Young girls, coming alone to a place like this for a holiday, very often change their minds. They go to different hotels — having met a personable young man on the train. And even young wives with children. They may have trouble at home. It is easier to engage a lawyer to serve divorce-papers if the wife is staying away from home and already has custody of the child or children. So they give the address of one hotel and stay at another. There are fifty-eight to choose from. This is a task for the missing Persons Bureau, not for the police. I just have not got the staff for such nonsense. These young missing girls are probably thoroughly enjoying their holiday here, each one living in sin with some over-sexed student in one of those cheap flats above the shops in the promenade.'

He paused, took a deep breath and then continued.

'All these problems are brought here — but all seem to solve themselves with a little patience. What I mean to say is this — if the first reports have not been followed up, then what can I do officially? Where can I look? Where can I go? There are no clues. There is no evidence.'

The deep and majestic voice had lifted two notes with emotion and righteous indignation. M. Pinaud began to think that M. le Chef's opinion of this functionary was perhaps justified. His hard features were set and stern as he replied.

'There is always something one can do, M'sieu Dumont. I have some information for you. I came here to investigate these murders, but last night there was another kidnapping. Marie Lahaye, the niece of M. le Chef of the *Sûreté*, took the train from Paris which arrived here at seven-thirty. She did not arrive at the Golden Lion Hotel, where her uncle had booked her a room. I can assure you that a good deal will be done officially regarding this matter.'

'But — but — '

Dumont stared at him with a dismay and astonishment that seemed to have rendered him momentarily incapable of speech. M. Pinaud stood up from his chair.

'Right,' he said. 'I shall be in charge of both investigations, with full authority from the *Sûreté*, and I shall naturally count on your help and collaboration.'

Dumont had stood up as well.

'Of course, M'sieu Pinaud.'

'Now — is there anything else you wish to tell me?'

Dumont hesitated.

'Well,' he began slowly, 'There was just one thing — '

Then he paused.

'Come on, man — come on,' M. Pinaud prompted him impatiently. 'This is not going to be an easy one. Anything you think — anything that might help — '

This seemed to encourage Dumont considerably.

'Well, what I told you about clues and evidence still holds, but there are two characters here in this place who seem to have far more money to spend in the casino than is right. One is Correvon, the manager of the Golden Lion, who drinks far too much, and the other is Morelli, who owns the Casino on the promenade. This has a good reputation for honest dealing and therefore he must have some other source of income. I was going to make a few discreet enquiries myself. And they both have houses on top of the headland, quite near where the Mansard bodies were found. Mind you, these are only suspicions. As I said before, there are no clues and there is no evidence. They could not keep any kidnapped person in these houses — there are servants living in and they both entertain on a fairly lavish scale. But it is the money that worries me.'

'You are quite right,' M. Pinaud told him. 'Fifty thousand francs for each operation — and counting all the ones that have not been reported to you — makes quite a good income. I will see both of these gentlemen. Is there anything else?'

Dumont shook his head.

'Not at the moment. I will let you know.'

'Do that. Now — are the Mansard bodies still in the morgue?'

'Yes. The formalities are not yet completed.'

'Good. I will see them before I go. But first I must know where they were found. My car is outside — would you come with me and show me?'

'Of course, M'sieu Pinaud.'

★   ★   ★

He got in his car and started the engine. Dumont sat beside him.

'Turn right here,' he said. 'This promenade, which is reinforced in depth by small side streets behind, because the land is flat as far as the river, is the one main road here. Where you joined it from the N1 there is a headland with several large and expensive houses. It is an exclusive residential area — no holiday-makers allowed — a private road up one side and down the other, and a high fence at the edge of the cliff, with a sheer drop down into the sea. At low tide people can walk along the beach, but not when the tide is high.

'Is this the way you came in, M'sieu Pinaud — when you turned from the main road at the signpost?'

'Yes.'

'Right. Slow down now. There is an entrance soon to the private road with a sign. It makes an almost complete circle and has a very steep gradient — you will need a low gear.'

The sign was not vulgarly large, but clearly painted and unmistakable;

Strictly private
property
Trespassers will be
prosecuted

It was artistically framed in one of the two small copses of young trees which had been planted on either side of the private road.

'Slowly here. There is a reversing lane just ahead. You will have to use it — the bodies were found near. Unless you

61

wish to call now — '

M. Pinaud shook his hand, turned the car and stopped in the reversing lane.

'Not now,' he replied.

'Just as well,' said Dumont as he got out. 'I told you about Correvon and Morelli, who both live here. Then there is Lasalle, the bank manager of the *Credit Nord*. They will all be at work. There are three others, an elderly couple, a retired author and the schoolmaster with his family — but they are on holiday. It is not a large area — each house has its own garden. Oh — and there is a very old fisherman's cottage right on the edge by the fence. They decided to leave it when they built. I think the owner Madoule acts as caretaker when the residents go away.'

The place was a short distance beyond the reversing lane, beside the road and under an overhanging shelf of rock.

'It would seem that they wanted the bodies to be found,' said Dumont. 'No attempt at concealment. The tradesmens' vans come up here every morning early for deliveries. The first one's driver saw them and reported it. The vans all turn in front of the houses. I sent a squad-car with two policemen to tidy up and check for any clues. There was nothing — except some fresh oil stains on the land there, probably from the car or the truck they used.'

'Right,' said M. Pinaud as he turned back to his car. 'I will come back here later — after I have been to the station — and call on these people. One of them might have noticed or heard something on the night of the murders. Take me to the morgue now, if you please, Inspector Dumont. Then I will go to the Golden Lion. There should be a photograph and a description of Marie Lahaye waiting for me. I will take them to the station and have another talk with one of the porters there. He has some recollection of seeing a young girl with a suitcase getting in a taxi last night. Then tomorrow I am going back to Paris.'

'But — may I say this, M'sieu Pinaud — what good will that do? Even if a porter saw this — with twenty or thirty taxis waiting — how on earth can we find out the number? This is the busiest time of the year. Even if another passenger or family were next to her and saw her get in — why should they be interested? Their only concern would be to make sure of the next taxi in the queue. And even if someone took or remembered the number or the description and we questioned the driver — what then? If he were mixed up in this, he would obviously deny everything and swear that he had driven her straight to her destination, the Golden Lion hotel, which she would obviously have told him, and then gone home to his supper. What proof — what evidence would you have that he was lying? Anything might have happened after he drove away. She might have gone shopping — all the shops keep open late at the height of the season. Or to the Casino.'

'She promised to telephone me as soon as she arrived.'

'She might have met someone she knew and been delayed — or enticed round a corner into one of the side-streets off the promenade — there may be several explanations — '

He continued to talk, doubtless giving some more, but by now M. Pinaud was no longer listening. He was driving, at a dangerous speed, down a very steep hill. And he was thinking that it was not a task of insuperable difficulty to think up these and other equally futile explanations, all of which must have had a supreme appeal to one who was content to sit on his backside and meditate earnestly on their feasibility instead of getting up and doing something in order to find out the truth.

He thought as well that he would have to correct M. le Chef's choice of word. Idiot was not strong enough. His English friends had taught him a different and shorter one, far more appropriate and very much more descriptive.

★　★　★

Outside it had been warm with bright summer sunshine. M. Pinaud shivered as the cold refrigerated air of the morgue seemed to strike him like a physical blow.

A young attendant pulled back the

sheets which covered the two iron trays.

'According to one of our two local doctors,' said Dumont, 'who help us out when necessary, Mansard was stabbed with a very thin sharp knife and then run over several times, probably by a heavy truck. His daughter has only one wound, a blow on the back of the head. This fractured her skull and was the cause of death. She had been sexually assaulted before.'

Mansard's features were not recognisable. M. Pinaud fought back an impulse to be sick and looked at the daughter.

The small face was calm and composed, completely untouched, and ineffably poignant in repose. The purity of the faint lines from brow to cheek reminded him of the petals of a flower. It had been a face of laughing intelligence, alert and alive and eager. Now it was still and small, and sad and dead.

He stood there without moving, without speaking, sick and tired at the pity, the waste, the tragedy and the futility of it all. He remembered the letter that he had read, and rage convulsed him as he thought that there were men so vile that they were prepared to cause sin and shame and pain and suffering, and even death, for money.

He knew that he was trembling as he stood there, and he felt the slow aching tears surge up into his eyes, brim over and course down his cheeks, but he did not know that behind them there was the glow of an expression — compounded of a depth of emotion and an intensity of feeling — that caused Dumont, who had been watching him curiously, to hastily avert his own.

4

In the reception office of the Golden Lion M. Pinaud saw his friend Clarisse.

'Sorry to trouble you if you are busy,' he apologised politely, 'but I am expecting a special delivery — '

'That's right,' she interrupted with a cheerful smile, reaching for an envelope on the side of her desk. 'You must be an important man, M'sieu Pinaud. Special driver, special car all the way from the *Sûreté* and the Quai d'Orsay. I did not know what to do with it. You did not tell me where you were going.'

Her tone was reproachful.

'I am sorry,' he said meekly.

This then was the end of all his efforts to remain an unknown friend of the missing Marie Lahaye. By lunch-time everyone in the town of Rouplage would know who he was and what he was doing there. It would not help his investigation. The very people he wanted to find would be alerted. But it could not be helped. How could he hope to find her without this information?

But mingled with his annoyance and frustration was a sense of pride and gratitude for M. le Chef's fantastic efficiency. No-one knew better than he how trying the old bastard could be at times, but when the need was there he never let you down.

The inner door on the far side of the office opened suddenly and the manager Correvon ushered another man out politely.

This morning the man was sober and alert, although his eyes were still pouched and veined and bloodshot. When he saw M. Pinaud he hesitated and then, taking his companion by the arm, he led him firmly across to the counter.

'Good-morning, M'sieu Pinaud,' he said quietly. 'I hope your room was confortable?'

'Very comfortable indeed, thank you.'

'May I present my very good friend, M'sieu Morelli, who owns and manages our Casino here.'

Morelli, as perhaps was to be expected from his name, looked like a high-born Italian aristocrat. His two-piece summer suit had been cut by an artist, but its effect was rather spoiled by a large and flashy gold tie-pin, in the form of a snake's head with ruby eyes, in the middle of his tie. He was small, dark and slender, with a black moustache above very red lips and long and silky hair. He held out his hand. His smile was a charming one.

'Carlo,' continued Correvon without any change in the inflection of his voice, 'this is M'sieu Pinaud of the *Sûreté*, who has come to Rouplage on special business.'

They shook hands cordially and murmured the appropriate words.

'We are just on our way to the bar, M'sieu Pinaud,' Correvon continued. 'Would you care to join us in a drink?'

M. Pinaud did not hesitate.

'That is very kind of you, M'sieu Correvon,' he replied at once. 'May I ask you to be kind enough to defer it until the next time we meet? I have an urgent appointment now which I must keep. I only called in here to pick up this.'

And he gestured to the envelope in his hand. M. le Chef, seeking to implement his efficiency, had perhaps inadvertently impaired it by choosing an envelope imprinted with *Sûreté*, Quai d'Orsay and Official in thick black letters that could easily have been read from the adjoining bar.

Correvon seemed to wrench his eyes away from it with an effort.

'Of course,' he murmured politely.

'My apologies,' replied M. Pinaud, not to be outdone in politeness. 'Nice to have met you, M'sieu Morelli. I shall visit your Casino as soon as I can. Until the next time. Good-bye for now.'

And with that he turned and left them.

★ ★ ★

He parked his car in the centre of the forecourt, switched off the engine, lit a cigarette and watched the scene with interest.

A train had just arrived from Paris.

Passengers were already coming out from the entrance-hall under the archway. Some walked straight towards the other cars parked in the forecourt. A few moved to the far end of the entrance and waited. Others approached the rank of taxis. A long line of them were waiting, one behind the other, the leading one opposite the archway. They were all fitted with standard bodies and the makes seemed fairly evenly divided between Renault, Peugeot and Citroën.

An elderly couple, burdened with cases and holdalls, approached the leading one. Its driver was wearing dark glasses and a silk scarf, as did several of the others behind him. That would be because of the glare and the top sand blowing in from the beach on a high wind. He was reading a newspaper. He laid it down, shook his head and jerked a thumb over his shoulder at the one behind. Then he resumed his reading.

M. Pinaud watched him, absorbed in thought. The ash on his cigarette grew longer and dropped down on to his trousers, but he did not move.

An experienced taxi-driver would have no difficulty in calculating to the nearest *centime*, from the clothes his prospective clients were wearing, the exact amount he would be likely to receive from them as a tip. These two did not look very prosperous — only tired and old and anxious. Or he could have been waiting for a special passenger who had already telephoned him and reserved his taxi, not wishing to wait in a queue.

Or, he thought with a sudden thrill of excitement, he could have been one of those who waited until the first rush was over and then got out, went into the hall and on to the platform, to verify if there might be a young girl alone with a suitcase, still absorbed in looking at the postcards or buying cigarettes at the kiosk. It would all be so easy in the confusion and the bustle of a train arriving at a busy and popular seaside resort in the height of the season.

The taxi-driver folded his newspaper, started his engine and moved his taxi a short distance forward. Then he got out and went into the station. The remainder of the taxi queue advanced as the passengers continued to engage them.

M. Pinaud left his car and did the same. As he passed he memorised the registration number of the isolated taxi. Its driver was putting coins into the public telephone box beside the booking-hall. He was probably trying to find out from his employer if the client who had booked his taxi had missed the train and whether he should wait or come back for the next one. As Dumont had said, there was no proof and no evidence.

*　*　*

The platform by now was nearly empty. He found his red-faced porter with an assortment of old-fashioned valises, hold-alls and carpet-bags fastened to each end of a double strap over one massive shoulder, leaving his arm free to support a frail and elderly lady who still retained her clear and well bred voice and imperious manner.

'Are you quite sure you have got them all, my good man?' she was asking him as they made their way slowly towards the exit. From the expression on the porter's face the question must have already been asked several times before. 'I did ask you to count them carefully. There should be seven.'

'I did count them, madame. You are quite right. I have seven on my shoulder. And I checked your compartment, if you remember, while you waited for me. I can assure you that it is now quite empty.'

'Oh, thank you. Thank you so much.'

The man saw M. Pinaud and recognised him with a cheerful smile. But he did not stop.

'This way, madame, for the taxi. I will put your luggage in for you and the driver will carry it out when you get home.'

He shepherded her carefully into the hall. M. Pinaud waited patiently on the platform. At least his colleague — he of the monosyllabic conversation — was not with him, and therefore this should not take long.

When he re-appeared the porter was smiling even more cheerfully. Evidently the old lady had not only been grateful but generous as well.

'Good-morning, m'sieu.'

'Good-morning to you. I am glad you remember me.'

Mr Pinaud extracted a photograph and a typewritten sheet of paper from the envelope he held in his hand. He held out the photograph.

'This is the young lady I was asking about last night — the one who came here on the seven-thirty.'

He held it out to the porter and began to read from the paper.

'She wore a pale-blue two-piece costume with a white silk blouse. Small round straw hat with a brim. Also blue. Black patent leather shoes with rosettes on top. Hat, rosettes and suitcase all matching colours.'

There was no hesitation.

'Yes, m'sieu — it was that one. I remember her definitely. With this photo and the clothes, I can be quite sure. I did not go up to her — the suitcase was small. She could easily manage it herself. I prefer to wait for someone who cannot manage their luggage — as you saw just now. Means a bigger tip. I noticed your young lady because she was the quickest one off the train — she must have got the first taxi.'

'Thank you very much. You have been of great help.'

'You are welcome, m'sieu.'

M. Pinaud offered him a cigarette, which seemed to please him inordinately. He would have liked to make this obliging porter's day by adding to the old lady's tip, but M. le Chef had an infuriating habit of always querying such items on his expense-sheet as unnecessary, with the result that to save argument and to preserve his own peace of mind, he usually paid them out of his own pocket. The end of the month was too near for him to do such a thing now, so after a few moments of general conversation and another cigarette, he repeated his thanks, said good-bye and left him.

* * *

There was some considerable delay at the level-crossing, while an incompetent shunting driver made a shambles of coupling a goods-wagon on to the end of the train that was returning to Paris — a delay long enough, he thought afterwards, for one or even two telephone-calls. For by now, he realised bitterly, thanks to M. le Chef's official envelope with the photograph, everyone in Rouplage would know who he was. And his car, with its Parisian number-plates, would be unmistakable.

The barriers finally lifted and the traffic surged forward. He drove back to the promenade and then followed the same road to the headland that he had taken with Dumont earlier on.

He braked, changed down and swung the wheel for the turn into the private road.

And then suddenly the heavy truck shot out from behind the concealment of the young conifers and raced downhill straight at him deliberately in a roaring surge of power, accelerating violently on low gear.

His first and instinctive impulse was to avoid the collision. Years of experience and conditional reaction to emergencies made this natural. But in the same second, even as his hands tightened convulsively on the wheel and his foot swung to stamp the brake — such is the instantaneous wonder of thought — the logic of reason dominated instinct.

His thoughts were not successive — there was no time. He seemed to see them all simultaneously in the one flaring picture of his vision. This was deliberate. The truck was much heavier than his own car. And much older. The glass of the windscreen would not be laminated.

At the last split-second he jammed his foot down hard again on the accelerator, tore the wheel back the other way and drove straight into the truck.

His car was by no means as heavy as the other vehicle. But it was not a small one. And the powerful engine had been turning at high revolutions in low gear, which gave it quite a momentum.

There was a terrific shock and the rending crash of buckled and twisted metal. His own windscreen starred, but held. His safety-belt had stayed taut and saved him.

Deliberately and stiffly he unclasped it, climbed over the front seat and found one back door that would open. He got out and walked slowly around the back of the wreck that had once been his car.

He had been right about the wind-screen of the truck. It had shattered with the impact into a hundred slivers and splinters. One large, long and jagged piece was deeply embedded in the driver's throat. He was a dark and swarthy man and he was hanging dead in his safety-belt, his filthy and greasy overalls soaked with his own blood.

The sight was a gruesome one and affected M. Pinaud strongly. He realised that he was suffering from the reaction of delayed shock and therefore forced himself to do two things quickly.

First of all he took a somewhat prolonged swallow from his pocket-flask of brandy. Secondly he verified that there was no chance of fire breaking out. His own radiator had taken most of the impact, since the truck was higher than his car, his carburettor was well back and his petrol-tank at the rear. The tank of the truck was mounted on two girders at the side, but the massive iron transverse bar across the front that had caused most of the damage to his own car had shielded it from damage. He disconnected both batteries, waited a few more moments to make sure and then set off up the hill to walk to the nearest house on the headland, where he could telephone to Dumont.

* * *

The walk and the fresh air did him good. By the time he was ringing the bell at the front door of the first house he felt almost completely recovered.

A pleasant middle-aged lady, dressed in a black gown and wearing a small white apron, was smiling at him.

'Yes, m'sieu?'

Her eyes were swollen and lined, but neither saddened nor defeated, by sorrow. Her skin was wrinkled like a russet apple, but still pink with the bloom of good health.

'I am sorry to disturb you, madame, but would you be kind enough to allow me to use your telephone? There has been an accident at the end of your road and I would like to inform the police.'

'Of course, m'sieu. Please come inside. The telephone is here in the hall. Nothing serious, I hope?'

'Thank you. I am afraid it is. A man is dead.'

'Oh — how shocking. You are quite right to telephone. You will find the number of the *Préfécture* in the pad on the table.'

'Thank you once again, madame,' he replied, stepping into the hall. 'This is the house of — '

'M'sieu Correvon, of the Golden Lion hotel, lives here. But naturally he is there now.'

'Of course. Actually I am staying in his beautiful hotel. I came here on business from Paris. Are you alone here, Madame — '

'Boucheron — Madame Boucheron. Oh no — I am his housekeeper. We have two resident maids, both town girls. M'sieu Correvon is an extremely wealthy man and does a considerable amount of entertaining. Here is the telephone.'

'I am very much obliged to you.'

She walked out of the hall and closed a door firmly behind her.

M. Pinaud turned over the pages of the indexed pad with one hand and lifted the receiver with the other. He had a warrant and his credentials in his pocket, but as he dialled the number he reflected that it would hardly be worthwhile searching this house for a kidnapped girl. He liked and appreciated Madame Boucheron. In his opinion she was hardly the type to be involved.

★   ★   ★

'Hullo — Inspector Dumont?'

'Yes — speaking.'

'Pinaud here. I am telephoning from Correvon's house on the headland. A man in a truck tried to kill me or put me out of action about half-an-hour ago. He was waiting by the sign at the beginning of the cliff road, concealed by the trees, and drove straight out at me.'

Spluttering noises of astonishment came over the wire, followed by the question.

'What happened?'

'He tried to run into me — to put me out of action. I ran into him instead. He is dead.'

'Amazing — '

'Not at all. Someone obviously does not want me here investigating. Would you send up a tow-car to take him away as soon as possible, and find out from the registration number and his papers everything possible about him. The people he knew — those he was seen with — all the information you can get. This was very probably the truck that ran over Mansard.'

'Yes. I will do that.'

'Thank you. And then send another tow-car, or the same one, in about two hours, to pick up mine and bring me back to town. Since I am already here, I want to go on and have a look first at these houses and the people on the headland.'

'Right, M'sieu Pinaud. Leave it all to me.'

'Thank you. Good-bye.'

5

At the second house, which was larger, the lady wore a pale blue housecoat over her black dress. Her hair was grey, her features lined and tragic, and yet still fierce and aggressive.

'Yes?'

She did not smile, so he smiled for her. His manner was extremely polite.

'I am sorry to disturb you, madame, but I understand that one of these houses here is for sale. Could I ask you — '

'No,' she interrupted him with great determination, 'This is the establishment of M'sieu Morelli, who owns the Casino on the promenade. You will have to speak to him. He will be here from six o'clock until eight this evening. He has given strict instructions to all the staff here not to answer any questions.'

'The staff being — ' he prompted gently and encouragingly, ignoring her rudeness.

'Myself — the housekeeper, the two maids, our cook and the butler.'

This information was volunteered with considerable pride.

'Thank you for your courtesy, madame,' he told her, his impassive features successfully concealing the irony of his sarcasm. 'I will ask him myself at the Casino to-night.'

Even though this house was larger than that of Correvon, he thought as he turned to leave, it was hardly likely that the cook would sleep with the butler. There would be no room for a kidnapped girl. If Dumont's suspicions were justified, it meant the complication of an accomplice in the town.

He then walked past the fisherman's old cottage, a small rectangular building with from what he could judge were immensely thick walls, set right on the edge of the fence-bounded cliff.

He decided to leave this one until last, and continued along the road to the next house, which was almost as large as Morelli's. But there no-one opened the door to his ring, and therefore he walked on.

The one after was smaller, but with a much larger garden. He had hardly removed his finger from the bell when the door was opened jointly by a charming elderly couple. They radiated the unmistakable satisfaction of two people who after a lifetime of marriage still found themselves so happy, contented and compatible that they continued to do everything together, even opening doors. This was so refreshingly unexpected that he decided on a different approach.

'Good-day to you, madame and m'sieu. My name is Pinaud, from the *Sûreté* in Paris. I am investigating the murder that took place, probably on this headland or somewhere near, a few days ago. The bodies of Mansard the local jeweller and his daughter were found on the road near here by one of the local tradesmen the following morning, three days ago.'

'Yes,' said the lady, looking at him curiously. 'We heard about that. What a dreadful thing. So many extraordinary types seem to come here to Rouplage for a holiday.'

He felt in his pocket and produced his credentials, which obviously seemed both to impress and please them. The man held the door open wider.

'You had better come inside, M'sieu Pinaud,' he said.

'Thank you.'

They led him into a small but beautifully furnished sitting room.

'Our name is Andressin,' said the lady.

'But there is not very much that we can tell you,' added her husband.

Throughout the interview they each spoke in rotation, one after the other. The sequence never varied — first one and then the other. He found this strangely and poignantly moving.

He stood beside the chair they had indicated and waited courteously until they were both seated. This also seemed to please them both.

'Well, now,' he began, 'it is the evening or the night before the bodies were discovered that is important. Did you hear or see anything unusual?'

It was Mme Andressin's turn. Her husband waited politely.

'We did not actually see anything — '

'But then it was dark — '

'And there is no point in looking out of the windows at the garden — '

'But we did hear a most peculiar noise — '

'It was quite late — '

'After the guests had gone from M'sieu Correvon's house — '

'And M'sieu Morelli's as well — '

'It sounded like a heavy truck or tradesman's van — '

'Being driven forwards and back-wards — '

'In the same place — '

'Because the noise of the engine did not increase or diminish — '

'It did not last very long — '

'We thought perhaps someone had got stuck in the reversing lane — it is very narrow — '

'But tradesmen only call in the morning — '

'Never at that time of night — '

'Never.'

M. Pinaud's head had been turning politely from one to the other. Neither of them had once spoken out of turn.

This was not evidence, nor was it proof, but it was confirmation of what they already knew. There was no point in distressing these charming people with the revolting details of Mansard's body in the morgue. And he knew instinctively that it would be a waste of time to search this small house.

So he stood up and thanked them both very sincerely for their information.

'You have been most helpful,' he assured them. 'This is valuable confirmation, since the bodies were found quite near the reversing-lane. Good-day to you both. I must go now. I have other calls to make.'

They both shared the opening of the front door and he left them smiling delightedly at each other.

* * *

There remained only two more houses apart from the cottage, one larger than the other. As he walked up the path of the larger one, the door of the other opened and a stentorian voice boomed across the intervening garden space.

'Don't waste your time, my dear fellow. That pompous old fool Lasalle is in his bank and at this time of the afternoon Madame takes her nap and would not come down for the President himself. Come in and have a drink.'

He looked at his watch and realised that the owner of the voice was right. It was three o'clock in the afternoon and he had not eaten any lunch. It might not be wise to drink on an empty stomach, but there was no denying the fact that it would be an extremely pleasant thing to do.

He retraced his steps and walked towards the man in the doorway. He was a striking figure, tall and gaunt, of late middle-age with greying hair badly in need of a cut. He wore a shabby but clean white shirt and even shabbier trousers. His features were deeply lined, his eyes dark and intense, humorous and sympathetic, and his smile infectious.

'Come in — come in,' he said, stepping to one side of the open door. 'You are just in time for a drink. I am Jean Randon, unsuccessful author. From my study window upstairs I have watched your progress all over the headland with interest and curiosity. You don't look like the man who reads the meters. You can't be selling anything — you have no samples. You might be — '

M. Pinaud held up his hand and laughed.

'You are wasting your valuable drinking time, M'sieu Randon. My name is Pinaud, from the Paris *Sûreté*. I am investigating your murders. Your remark is the most sensible one I have heard to-day. I accept with pleasure.'

'Good — good — come inside then. Take a chair.'

He was ushered into a small dining-room. Randon walked straight to the sideboard against the far wall and busied himself with bottles and glasses, but he never stopped talking.

'I can't tell you how pleased and delighted I am to see a different face for a change. You look a respectable and intelligent type — in contrast to most of my bloody awful neighbours. We really have a shower up here. Correvon and Morelli are not my type. The two turtle-doves are still in love after fifty years of marriage and are only interested in continuing their romance. Lasalle the banker is also a town councillor and President of the local Chamber of Commerce. You know the type — there is no need to say any more. Madoule — the gypsy in the cottage — I would not trust further than I can kick him — '

M. Pinaud had been watching him in awed fascination. Randon, all the while he had been talking, had taken two huge tumblers, put in cubes of ice and twists of lemon-peel and was now pouring generously an incredible mixture of Campari and Scotch whisky. He thought that he must be dreaming. But to dream one must be asleep. Therefore he must be having hallucinations. But the labels on the bottles were unmistakable.

'The gypsy?' he interrupted. Perhaps if he spoke himself it would confirm that he was neither sleeping nor dreaming nor having hallucinations.

'Yes — the nasty one in the cottage.'

Randon answered but did not stop pouring.

'But I was told that it was a fisherman's — '

'When it was built, maybe — in the days of Louis the Fourteenth. But he is no more a fisherman than my arsehole. Pure-blooded gypsy.'

He came back to the other chair in front of the table with a glass in each hand.

'It is all my fault, I suppose. I bought this place for peace and quiet. That was in the days when I thought I would be famous.'

He laughed, shortly and hardly. Then he took a huge swallow from his glass.

'Your very good health, M'sieu Pinaud.'

'Thank you. And yours too.'

M. Pinaud drank, with perhaps a little more caution. Separately, yes. Before and after meals, certainly. But never before together.

'May I say that in what amounts to practically a lifetime of serious drinking, I have never — '

A great bellow of laughter interrupted him.

'I know what you are going to say — I am not surprised. I invented it myself. What do you think of it?'

'Well — '

He hesitated.

'It certainly is most unusual — '

Once again Randon laughed. He took another great swallow.

'Yes — you can say that. And it has a delayed action that is fantastic. Something like the kick of a mule. Inspires me to write.'

'Then I must be careful. I have to work.'

'Of course — I forgot. Our murders. I am afraid I can't help you. I only know what the milkman told me. My wife will be furious that she missed it all. She has gone to visit our daughter and the new baby. Back to-morrow. Women seem to go mad over babies — I can't think why. It is an abnormal reaction to the straightfor-ward biological purpose for which they were designed and evolved — why make a fuss? I think personally that the creating of one is far more worthy of attention.'

M. Pinaud could not think of any intelligent comment to make on this somewhat unorthodox opinion, and therefore contented himself with taking another modest sip of this extraordinary concoction and changing the subject.

'You introduced yourself, M'sieu Randon, as an unsuccessful author. May I ask — '

'Of course. Why not?'

He stood up, his glass empty in his hand.

'But you are not drinking — '

'Thank you — I still have plenty. And more work to do.'

'As you wish.'

Randon walked over to the sideboard to re-fill his glass and began to speak over his shoulder as he did so.

'I decided to become an author the last year I was at school. The year I failed my examination to the University. With my usual luck I had a severe *migraine* at the time of the most important paper. I took various jobs afterwards — nine o'clock until six — and wrote every evening and week-ends. Sometimes even before break-fast. Then I had the first one published. That was the day. I had wonderful and eulogistic reviews — full of praise — from the most eminent literary critics. I cut them all out and pasted them into a huge notebook.'

He came back to his chair with the glass full in his hand. He sat down and continued to drink and talk.

M. Pinaud drank a little more, very carefully. After all, from what he remembered, one drank such quality whisky — the label was world-renowned — neat with coffee, or with ginger-ale or soda-water. It was Campari that took the lemon and perhaps a little gin. Was it the proportion that had been wrong? A little less whisky and a little more Campari — would that have helped? He became aware that Randon was speaking.

'And of course I was inspired and encouraged to go on writing. You can have no idea — if you are not an author — of the ecstatic and childishly egoistical delight there is in signing free copies of your own book and presenting them benevolently to all your friends and relations.

'I went on writing. I had more books published. I changed my job — several times. I met my wife. We got married. I wrote more books. And every one inevitably seemed to get better and more enthusiastic reviews. I had to buy two more notebooks to stick them all in.'

He paused and looked sadly at his glass. It was nearly empty. Then he looked up. M. Pinaud wondered what he could see.

'But I never made any money. I had film options which came to nothing. Lack of finance. I had foreign translation rights which ceased after the first edition. I never had intensive advertising. But I went on writing. I am still writing — after fifty published books. Last week I bought another notebook for my reviews. We saved up to buy this house, for peace and quiet. Now we have a murder — and I know nothing about it. And neighbours I can't stand.'

M. Pinaud made a great effort and finished his drink. Then he stood up and held out his hand.

'Another one for the road?' asked Randon.

'No, thank you. I have had enough. A most remarkable drink, and may I say extremely welcome. Thank you for your hospitality, M'sieu Randon, and your most interesting conversation. The most important part of it, in my opinion, is the fact that you are still writing. That, to an author, is the only significant thing. Which makes your description of yourself as unsuccessful completely wrong to me. May I wish you, very sincerely, the courage and the inspiration to continue and good luck?'

Randon's words of thanks were a whisper, broken with emotion and intense feeling.

It might have been genuine emotion, reflected M. Pinaud as he walked with great care down the path away from the house. It was a recognised and accepted fact that authors were notoriously strange, sensitive and incomprehensible people . . .

Or, on the other hand, it might have

been those diabolical drinks. He had consumed three.

One thing was certain. It was hardly likely that the husband of a wife who was normal enough to take a delight in her daughter's baby would be a kidnapper.

* * *

It was only a short walk to the cottage, but his mind raced furiously in thought with every step he took.

This might all be a lot of nonsense. He was probably — almost certainly — wasting his time. The bodies had been taken to the headland simply to ensure that they would be found early in the morning. This was a deserted and convenient spot. In the town there would have been far too many holiday-makers still walking about late at night.

The fact that Dumont's prime suspects both lived here did not mean a thing. One could hardly conceal a kidnapped girl in a house with a resident staff. Then where had they been hidden — if Dumont were right? There were hundreds of houses in

Rouplage. Where could he begin to look?

The cottage was a plain rectangular structure, with immensely thick flint walls and three dilapidated out-buildings added on to one end.

He lifted the heavy iron knocker and let it fall on a round stud set in the wide-planked door. It opened almost immediately and he looked at the soft brown eyes of Madoule the gypsy. He had the swarthy and leathery skin of his race and a high forehead with receding black hair. He wore a shirt and trousers tucked into high boots.

M. Pinaud was inclined to agree with the author's opinion. This one he would not trust. The brown eyes, in spite or perhaps even because of their softness, were inscrutable.

'Good-afternoon to you, M'sieu Madoule. My name is Pinaud, from the Paris *Sûreté*. Here are my credentials. I am investigating the two murders you had up here the other day and trying to find another young girl who was kidnapped at the station last night. I understand from Inspector Dumont that you act as caretaker for the residents up here when they go away. I have a warrant here to search your cottage and the one empty house. You have the keys, I presume?'

'Yes.'

There was no surprise, no emotion, no expression at all in the brown eyes as the man stepped back and held the door open wide.

'I saw you come up and call on everyone,' he added.

'No doubt — if you were watching. This is the highest point on the headland. Do you wish to see my warrant?'

Madoule shook his head.

'There is no need. I have nothing to hide.'

'Good.'

M. Pinaud stepped inside. There were two small rooms on the ground floor, with an immense open double fireplace to heat both connecting them, flanked by two narrow planked doors. This first one was obviously used as a kitchen and was fitted with a sink and a small oven.

Madoule opened one of the doors and showed him the other room, plainly and cheaply furnished. The other half of the enormous fireplace was identical. On a small table beneath the window was a telephone.

M. Pinaud gestured towards it.

'That is unusual — for a cottage like this, surely? I did not see any poles — '

'Underground,' the man interrupted briefly. 'No poles would ever stand up to the gales we get here in the winter. That explains the telephone. Sometimes we have to telephone for supplies and walk to the other road to collect them. This one gets blocked with snow-drifts.'

'I see.'

A steep mediaeval ladder, made from two young tree trunks and split logs, led up from the corner of the room to a square opening in the ceiling.

M. Pinaud climbed first, Madoule followed. Here were two more rooms. The first was a bedroom, with a single iron bed, a wardrobe and a dressing-table. The second was empty except for several old and disused pieces of furniture stacked up at one end. The connecting door was the only one on the upper floor. There were no ceilings; the vast beams that supported heavy planks underfoot were clearly visible as were the acutely angled ones and the joists of the steep and narrow roof. Both of these rooms were also much smaller than one would have expected.

When they came down the ladder M. Pinaud commented on this.

'It is the thickness of the walls,' Madoule replied indifferently. 'They knew how to build in those days. Not like these other ones around here. This cottage will still be standing when they have all fallen down.'

He walked across the kitchen to the back door, taking a bunch of keys as he went from a nail in the wall.

'Three out-houses,' he said over his shoulder. 'Toilet, woodshed and tools.'

M. Pinaud conscientiously followed him into all three. The woodshed was literally crammed full of logs of different shapes and sizes, all sawn, split, sorted and stacked with beautiful precision. The tools were rusty and the toilet was dirty.

He thought again, as they walked together towards the empty house, that all this was indeed a lot of nonsense.

And after Madoule had used his keys and shown him all over a large and very luxuriously furnished and obviously empty house — not forgetting the loft, the cellar and the two garages — he saw no reason to change his opinion.

He waited while the man carefully relocked the front door.

'Thank you very much, M'sieu Madoule,' he said politely, 'For all the trouble you have taken and the help you have given me. I am only sorry that it has all been for nothing. But we have got to check. It is the only way.'

He did not offer to shake hands. There was something about this individual — he did not know what — that somehow seemed to repel him.

For the first time he could see some expression in the soft brown eyes. It was a sly and cunning one.

'Very pleased to help, M'sieu Pinaud,' he said. 'You have seen how and where I live. Quite simply. Not like some on this headland. But we Romany folk know things other people don't.

'What sort of things?'

'Things that doctors don't.'

'Such as?'

'A verruca. Have you ever had a verruca under your foot?'

'Yes,'

'What did you do?'

'Went to a doctor and had it cut out.'

'Nonsense. It only comes back.'

'What would you do?'

'Banana-skin without the banana. Heat it, bind it on and put the sock on top. Two days and the verruca has gone — for good.'

'That is remarkable. It is kind of you to tell me. I must go now — I am already late. Thank you once again. Good-bye, M'sieu Madoule.'

★ ★ ★

The tow-car was already in position as he arrived at the end of the private road, with his own car rearing up pathetically on the end of the hoist. The driver was sitting behind the wheel, smoking a cigarette and not troubling to conceal the fact that he was tired, bored and impatient.

A polite young policeman hastened to meet him and saluted smartly.

'Inspector Dumont's compliments, m'sieu. He would have come himself, but he thought his time would be better spent finding out about the truck-driver.'

'Quite right. I am sorry to have made you wait. I will be in touch with him.'

'Do you mind coming in the front? There is room for three.'

'Not at all.'

The driver growled a greeting and spat out his cigarette. Then he started the engine, shifted the gear-lever, let in his clutch and roared off at a dangerous speed, with M. Pinaud's car following valiantly if somewhat pathetically on its rear wheels.

'Where would you like to go, M'sieu Pinaud?'

'Anywhere near the Golden Lion will do for me, thank you.'

'We pass it.'

'Good.'

They were soon there. M. Pinaud

thanked them both with great sincerity and got out on to the pavement. The tow-car roared off at once. For a moment he stood there, motionless in the midst of the swarming people, and sighed as he watched how obediently his own car followed it.

Then he walked to the entrance-doors of the Golden Lion and went inside the hotel.

6

He lay back in the delightful relaxation of a large bath almost filled with very hot water, blissfully content.

He had ascertained from his friend Clarisse, as soon as he came in, that there was positively no possibility of getting anything to eat before seven o'clock. That was the rule of the hotel. On the other hand, if he presented himself a little earlier and spoke very nicely and persuasively to the head waiter, who would then speak even more nicely and even more persuasively to the cook, there was always the chance that he might begin with the soup before the others. The soup had to be made first, naturally, and then kept hot.

By now he and Clarisse were firm friends. He was a man of great importance, the recipient of secret official documents, and here on a vital mission.

He meditated as he soaked tranquilly in

the bath, adding a little more hot water as it cooled, feeling almost physically the strains and the tensions of the shock and the fear of the crash all draining out of his body.

It had been an exhausting and perhaps a frustrating day. But there was no doubt that he was on the right track. Perhaps the porter had talked about him too much. Perhaps Marie Lahaye had taken the first taxi — the one that did not drive her to the Golden Lion. Then where had she gone? His afternoon on the headland had not been encouraging — and yet someone had wanted to put him out of action before he even started investigating. Why? The cottage was the only likely place up there and he had searched that thoroughly enough. There would have been difficulty in concealing a cat, let alone a human being.

Madoule looked the type who would sell his grandmother if the price were right. All the others seemed respectable enough. Either Correvon or Morelli might be implicated, if Dumont's suspicions were correct, but then where had they hidden Marie Lahaye? Perhaps the truck driver was the connecting link. But, in all fairness, to establish such a connection was not something Dumont could do in a hurry.

His meditations, he reflected ruefully, did not seem to be making much progress. He turned the tap to run in some more hot water and reached for the soap. How could any normal man be capable of constructive thinking on an empty stomach?

He was more than hungry. He was starving.

★   ★   ★

Perhaps it was that which made him so eloquent when he sat down at a corner table in the empty restaurant. Although his faithful chronicler had always maintained that when in the right mood he could talk the hind leg off an elephant. In that case starvation must undoubtedly have been one of the right moods.

Talk nicely, Clarisse had told him.

He did more than talk nicely. He

expounded and recounted. He described and explained. He charmed and flattered, he pleaded and convinced. And — not surprisingly — he triumphed.

The accident with the truck — enlivened by slight embellishments that precluded any thoughts of attempted murder — and the description of his interview with Randon, the unsuccessful author — during which they finished both the bottles of whisky and Campari — became epics of entertainment for weeks on end, even to the kitchen-maids while washing up.

He was on his third plate of soup, with only a crust of the long French bread remaining in its basket, by the time the first couple came in from the bar.

The omelette *aux fines herbes* was delicious. A masterpiece.

The praise he wrote on a page torn from his notebook which he asked the waiter to give personally to the cook was another masterpiece in its own right — a blend of courteous and restrained thanks, eloquent admiration, and the professional appreciation of a *gourmet*.

The cook was a man who took both his profession seriously and a justifiable pride in his work. It is therefore not surprising to relate that very shortly another omlette was unobtrusively placed in front of M. Pinaud, which gave the other diners, who were now coming into the restaurant in greater numbers, a fairer and more sporting chance of catching up with him.

On the wine-list he had recognised a name he knew well — a white wine from the shore of *Lac Léman* in Switzerland. One bottle was on his table, the other in the ice-bucket. He had ordered two — knowing full well that M. le Chef would only allow the dinner on his expense-sheet — because he felt in the mood to celebrate. This was an occasion worthy of celebration. Today he had escaped death by a miracle. Each time he raised his glass and drank, he closed his eyes and whispered a prayer of thankfulness with devout recognition and humility.

The fillet steak was immense, thick, underdone to perfection and so tender that it seemed to melt in his mouth.

He glanced at the couple who had first come in. While he had been writing his note and eating the second omlette they had caught up with him. Their steaks were not nearly as large as his.

He decided not to write any more notes to the cook. The cheese-board of the Golden Lion had a reputation which extended as far as Paris. And he was inordinately fond of cheese. Enough was as good as a feast.

Although he knew very well that it was the normal procedure to eat cheese immediately after the main course and any sweet, ice or fruit afterwards, he asked the waiter if he would be kind enough to bring him his *sorbet* first, so that he could have the satisfaction of completing such a magnificent meal, with the aid of this stupendous cheese-board, in a truly worthy manner.

Then he contemplated the cheese-board brought to his table by a smiling waiter with a great and profound satisfaction, knowing that his decision had been a wise one. There were large pieces of all his favourite cheeses, including a whole Thom and a noble-looking slab of Gruyère from Switzerland.

Swiftly he cut portions of these first, then of the Brie, the Camembert, the Roquefort, the Gorgonzola and the Stilton. Halfway through this operation the waiter, his smile even broader, handed him another plate from the sideboard. He must have overheard some of the conversation in the kitchen when he went out for the cheese-board.

M. Pinaud thanked him gravely, but did not relax his concentration on what he was doing. This was an operation which demanded undisturbed attention and undivided concentration. The portions he cut were not all of the same size. There were naturally his special favourites and then there were, amongst that magnificent selection, those he had neither seen nor tasted for a very long time. He concluded — since there was still a space on the second plate — by trying two he had never even seen before.

After all, this was a celebration. And the second bottle of that superb wine was still in the ice-bucket. He cut a slice of

Gruyère and tasted its strong richness with delight. Then he contemplated the two plates in front of him with a profound satisfaction. This was truly a noble ending to a magnificent meal. If he should need another bottle of wine to finish their contents he could always order one . . .

★   ★   ★

Later on that evening M. Pinaud stood in the entrance to the Casino on the promenade and stared in amazement.

It consisted of one enormous rectangular room, in the centre of which, under a vast hanging bowl-light, stood a roulette table, surrounded by the chairs of the players. Only the *croupier* stood. There were separate bars in two separate corners. Several smaller tables occupied most of the remaining space, with seated groups of people playing cards. To and from these tables hurried white-jacketed waiters with trays, their bases the corner bars. The walls were covered with gambling coin machines of every description. The *décor* was unbelievable — silver paint with strips of aluminium foil wherever there was enough space to put them.

The room was immense, but the number of people inside made it seem small. Their clothes were astonishing. Each person, male or female, wore what he or she considered eminently suitable for a place of entertainment at a seaside resort in the evening.

The result was fascinating. There must have been an astonishing divergence of opinion as to what was implied by the word suitable. There was everything from shorts, shirts and beach trousers to full evening gowns and dinner jackets.

Whatever their clothes, they were all noisy, hearty, loaded with drink and thoroughly enjoying themselves. And whatever the clothes, the person inside them, by a certain brash aggressiveness of demeanour, made it quite clear that the correct choice of wear for a gambling Casino in holiday time was never a difficult problem — and besides, one always felt so happily correct by being suitably clothed . . .

M. Pinaud walked carefully between the bodies until he came to the roulette table. He saw that Morelli was the *croupier* and recognised Correvon in one of the chairs. The manager was in the same state as the night before, slightly and aggressively drunk. His pouched and dissipated eyes were glued on the wheel.

M. Pinaud came nearer and stood behind the chair of one of the players on the opposite side of the table.

Morelli leaned forward, spun the wheel and sent the ball skimming in the groove with an expert twist of his wrist.

'*Rien ne va plus*,' he called.

The ball spun clicking along the tines beside the numbers, slowed, jumped and finally came to rest.

'*Le numéro vingt-sept*,' Morelli intoned. '*Rouge, troisième douzaine, manque, impair*.'

With his rake he pulled in all the money along the green baize, leaving only the stake on number twenty-seven. Sighs, groans, oaths and laughter came from the seated players. Only Correvon stood up, waved to Morelli and threaded his way unsteadily towards the bar in the corner.

M. Pinaud watched his progress thoughtfully. It was strange that he should prefer to spend his time here instead of staying in the hotel where he could have enjoyed that magnificent meal without having to pay for it. Strange that he should wish to gamble in these garish surroundings rather than relax in that austere and beautiful dining-room, so eminently worthy of the food it provided.

Strange — and yet understandable. The urge to gamble was compulsive, as strong as the urges other men had to drink and fornicate, or molest small children. Understandable, even though he did not gamble himself. He did not mind taking a risk or accepting a chance, but he had never seen any point in betting on the turn of a card or the spin of a wheel. Perhaps because — in spite of his famous and celebrated exploits — his salary had never been enough to pay for all the things he had always wanted to buy for his wife and children . . .

'Good-evening, M'sieu Pinaud.'

Another play had ended, and he

became aware that Morelli was speaking to him.

'I beg your pardon — I was thinking. Good-evening to you, M'sieu Morelli. Business seems to be good.'

Morelli laughed.

'This is the season. This is when we try to make enough to pay for our idleness in the winter. But you have chosen the wrong night for your visit. I am on duty, as you see. Any other night I would have been pleased to show you around. Would you care to join us in the play?'

'No, thank you. If you will forgive me, I would sooner just watch. I am sorry, but I have had an exhausting day, and I have to catch the early train to Paris in the morning.'

'I am sorry too. Perhaps another night.'

The words were polite, but their tone indifferent and perfunctory. Morelli had already seen two couples take the empty chairs and immediately became all business.

'*Faîtes vos jeux, mesdames et messieurs — faîtes vos jeux.*'

M. Pinaud stayed watching for a little

longer. The stakes were high — extremely high — but that was no crime. It was to be expected. People on holiday usually brought plenty of money with them for amusement and entertainment and did not spend the evening in a Casino unless they enjoyed gambling. The play seemed to be honest and efficiently run.

To an onlooker, he was only watching the wheel with an absorbed interest. In reality, his eyes did not even see it. He was thinking.

He was thinking that he was not really interested in all these gambling holiday-makers. They could not possibly be implicated in local murders and kidnappings. Quite a large proportion of them had never been in Rouplage before. He had only come to this place to watch Correvon and Morelli.

What Morelli had said made sense. He was obviously making a fortune now in the height of the season with a well run and efficient Casino which many people clearly liked to patronise. But to run a place like this efficiently must cost a great deal of money. And in the winter months the bills would continue to come in. If his staff were good and if his other *croupier* was to be trusted, such people would not accept a six months contract. He would have to guarantee their employment on a yearly basis. Which was expensive, but the only way to operate and succeed.

He might have been thinking and Morelli may have been convinced that he was watching the play, but in spite of doing both he managed to keep an eye on Correvon, who was drinking at the bar.

He remembered the expression of utter despair in the manager's eyes as he had left the table after watching his stake being swept away by Morelli's rake. He remembered his boasting, the first night they had met, that he had plenty of money. And he remembered the man's unconcern and indifference regarding the non-arrival of a guest who had booked her room in his hotel — an attitude of mind difficult to reconcile with his position as manager. Unless he had something to hide.

No-one watching M. Pinaud would

ever have thought that he saw immediately when Correvon left the bar. His session there had been of little help to his unsteadiness. Indeed, his progress towards the door might never have terminated had it not been for the kindly and indulgent help of some of the holiday-makers, who not only willingly offered an arm, but obviously saw nothing reprehensible in anyone getting happily inebriated while on holiday.

M. Pinaud waited, apparently absorbed only in watching the roulette-wheel. He did not wish to follow him out. He was the type of individual who would disturb the well-deserved rest of that superb cook without compunction and order him to prepare another magnificent meal.

Perhaps Inspector Dumont was not such an idiot as M. le Chef had thought.

7

The next morning M. Pinaud took the early train to Paris and a taxi to the Quai d'Orsay.

He knocked on the door of the office on the first floor with some trepidation, remembering from the past how M. le Chef took a very poor view of operatives who had their cars smashed up, whatever the reason.

'Come in.'

He did so.

'Glad to see you, Pinaud.'

'Thank you, m'sieu.'

There was a smile on M. le Chef's face. What a pity to think how soon it would disappear. But it would be better to eradicate it at once with his bad news, rather than delay and thereby probably increase the impact of his anger later on.

'I am sorry to have to tell you, m'sieu, that my car is badly damaged. Yesterday a heavy truck was waiting, concealed behind some trees, and then driven — deliberately — straight at me. The object of the exercise was to put me out of action. Which means that I am on the right track. I must be making enough progress to be a nuisance.'

He stopped and looked across the desk in amazement. The smile was still there. Perhaps he was dreaming. Perhaps the old man was getting a little deaf and would not admit it. He made his voice slightly louder and a good deal clearer, so that his next words might help to placate him.

'May I thank you, m'sieu, for your invaluable help with the photograph and description — and the speed with which you sent them. I have already spoken with the porter at the station who positively identifies her. She definitely did arrive at Rouplage on the seven-thirty train.'

He paused. The smile was still there, even broader.

'No need to worry about the car, Pinaud. As you say, it is an encouraging sign. I will organise another one from the pool before you leave. There are other and more important things to think about just now'.

He picked up two sheets of notepaper from his desk and held them out. M. Pinaud stepped forward and took them,

'Here this morning — express post and special delivery.'

He recognised both the handwriting and the paper as he read them. The first one was similar but not quite the same as the one to Mansard.

We are very careful to treat our guests with every consideration at first while the money is being found. Naturally there can be no contact, only isolation, and a mask is worn when food is brought in.

If the money is not paid on demand, then we have other outlets for our merchandise and the organisation to ensure that no clues are ever left.

Your niece is older than Mansard's daughter, physically attractive and also a virgin. In certain of our markets these qualifications can ensure a very high price — far more than the ransom we are asking you. It would be far more sensible to pay.

The second one was practically the same.

Leave fifty thousand francs in a plain sealed envelope on the exit end of the central table in the Post Office at Rouplage at eleven o'clock precisely on Saturday the 22nd. Go straight out and walk away. You will be watched all the time. Your niece, Marie Lahaye, will be returned, safe and unharmed, to the Golden Lion hotel.

He looked up from his reading and handed the letters back.

'Yes, m'sieu. These are practically the same as the two Dumont showed me. He found them in Mansard's desk when he went through his papers. Same disguised handwriting. Same cheap untraceable paper.'

M. le Chef leaned back in his chair. The smile had disappeared. His features were now set and stern. And old and tired.

'Yes, Pinaud,' he said quietly. 'I am afraid that the torment of the last two nights, after you telephoned, and the relief of these letters this morning, almost closed my mind to the fact that you are investigating a murder case. I am very fond of my niece — even more since her mother died. She was my only sister. Now then — how are you getting on?'

'I think I am making some progress, m'sieu. This is proved by the fact that someone tried to kill me or put me out of action yesterday.'

'Where is he now?'

'He is dead. I realised that it was an old truck and took a chance on it having an old windscreen. So I accelerated instead of braking. That is why my car is in such a mess.'

M. le Chef looked at him very thoughtfully for quite a long time. But all he said was:

'Then to find out anything about him and who paid him will be more difficult and take longer.'

'Yes. But I had no choice. He was going downhill fast and the truck was a heavy one with an iron bar across the front. If I had braked I would not have had a chance.'

'Have you got Dumont on it?'

'Yes. He is trying to find out. I shall see him to-night or to-morrow.'

'Good.'

'I told you I spoke to one of the porters who recognised her photograph. She definitely arrived there. He said that she was the first one off the train. I watched an earlier one come in and saw the line of waiting taxis. The leading one refused a fare, telling them, I suppose, that he was engaged. I thought how easy it would be for him to wait until a young girl appeared alone with a suitcase, and then perhaps he would not have been engaged.

'But, as Dumont pointed out, there is no evidence. If we question him he will deny everything or else swear that he took her to her destination. I took his number. I intend to watch him again. He might have been the one who took your niece — not to the Golden Lion — but where?'

'Yes — where? That is the question. Do you think she will know anything?'

He shook his head.

'They cannot afford to take such a chance. She was probably drugged or blindfolded before being taken somewhere else.'

'Yes — but where?'

Again M. Pinaud shook his head.

'That is the problem. I went to all the houses yesterday on the headland where the bodies were found. I searched one empty one — the owners are on holiday — with the keys the caretaker had. I even searched the caretaker's cottage, but there was nothing. Your niece may have been taken anywhere in the town and the Mansard bodies brought back there to be found quickly.'

M. le Chef sat in silence for a moment, as if considering all the implications of what Mr Pinaud had told him. Then he sighed.

'It is not easy,' he said.

'That is the under-statement of the year,' M. Pinaud told him. 'Dumont informed me that he has two suspects

— Correvon, the manager of the Golden Lion, and Morelli, the owner of the local Casino. Correvon is an inveterate gambler and both men seem to spend more money than they could be expected to earn. Fifty thousand francs is quite a sum for one operation, and according to Dumont there have been other cases of disappearance reported to him. But they were never followed up, he said, so he assumed that the money had always been found. This case of the Mansards is the first time there has been any violence. He must have found out something or obtained some proof which they could not allow to be known. I say they — but I do not know how many are involved. If it is one man who organises the whole operation he must have accomplices.'

'I agree with you. What did you think of Dumont?'

M. Pinaud thought swiftly. It was a pity that he could not use the word his English friends had taught him, but M. le Chef, in spite of his remarkable sex-life, had inherited all the courtesy, the restraint, the good manners and the inhibitions of a well-born former generation, and he would not have been pleased.

'I think you were quite right, m'sieu. A bit of an idiot. Definitely not the man for this problem. I should think he has been there in the same job for too long.'

'Yes. That is exactly what I thought. To-morrow, when we see Marie, she may have noticed something — she may have seen the one thing which will give us a clue.'

M. Pinaud did not think so. These people knew what they were doing. They had done it before, many times and always successfully. The whole operation had been brilliantly planned. But he did not say anything.

'After all,' M. le Chef continued, 'She is an intelligent girl. She had sense enough to give my name for the ransom. Her father would have been useless. I already have the money. To-morrow I will go to Rouplage as instructed, but you will be there as well to catch him. I will have to leave immediately. But you will be watching in the crowd or in a telephone-box to see who picks up the envelope. If they know who you are you must disguise yourself. Call in your flat on the way back and change your suit. And get a beard and tinted glasses. But do nothing in the Post Office. Just see who takes the envelope and follow him out.'

He leaned forward in his chair and continued with an even greater emphasis.

'And if by any chance that should fail, I have another plan.'

'Indeed? And what is that, m'sieu?'

But M. le Chef shook his head.

'Not now, Pinaud — not now. Come back here after lunch and I will tell you then.'

'But — '

M. le Chef held up his hand.

'It would have given me great pleasure to have had lunch with you, but I am compelled to see the Minister. Come back here at half-past two, Pinaud, and then I will explain everything. And there will be another car ready for you.'

★　★　★

At precisely half-past two M. Pinaud knocked on the door.

'Come in.'

He did so, and then stopped in amazement. M. le Chef was as usual seated at his desk. But beside it was a chair. There had never been a second chair in this beautiful office in all the years of his employment by the *Sûreté*. Always he and any other caller had had to stand. Now there was a chair, and sitting in it was a girl.

He looked at her with interest. She was well worth looking at. Her hair was dark, with an attractive wave, and cut quite short to the shape of her head and neck. Her eyes were brown, alert and alive with intelligence. Her features were beautiful. Her figure was worthy of them. She wore a plain skirt and a silk blouse, and looked very efficient and business-like.

Now all this, his faithful chronicler hastens to point out, took place in the days when M. Pinaud was young and exceptionally virile. And goes on to maintain — with justifiable dignity — that he is only telling the truth when he describes — even if somewhat poetically and fancifully — how at the very sight of her a red hot tide of lust seemed to course through his hero's veins with the pulse of his blood.

'Come in, Pinaud — come in.'

He realised that he had been standing there transfixed in the doorway. She was so lovely, so faultless. The very sight of her made him feel like a schoolboy. He hastened forward.

'This is Denise Roche, one of our special operatives. Denise — this is M'sieu Pinaud, our most celebrated detective.'

She gripped the arms of her chair as if to stand up, but in two strides he was in front of her, his hand outstretched, his rare smile transfiguring the hard strong lines of his face.

'Please do not get up, Mademoiselle Roche.' He had noticed, while they had been on the arms of the chair, that there were no rings on the small slim hands. 'I am very pleased to meet you. M'sieu here is flattering me.'

He stepped back to his usual position

in front of the desk.

'Nonsense,' said M. le Chef. 'Eighteen successful cases are a remarkable achievement. We all know that here. If your chronicler's publishers and their publicity departments would only extract their digits the whole world would know.

'Now then — to business. I got Denise in here early this morning before you came so that I could put her in the picture and tell her what we know about these kidnappings. Which is not very much. This will save time and repetition.'

He paused for a moment to look at the sheet of blank notepaper in front of him, in order to be quite sure that all his thoughts were neatly arranged in a logical sequence.

M. Pinaud waited patiently. He had heard of the Minister and his reputation. It must have been a good lunch. His own had consisted of a glass of wine and a sandwich, consumed in twelve minutes. He sighed and concentrated on what was being said.

'In my opinion this kidnapper — I will refer to him in the singular for the sake of clarity although obviously he must have accomplices — will try again, and very shortly.'

It was strange, M. Pinaud thought swiftly, how people tended to become didactic in their old age.

'He has had a remarkable run of success. He is now confident. Therefore he is bound to try again. He has punished one — swiftly and mercilessly — who obviously had found out something which would have exposed him, and by so doing has removed all danger from himself. Now he has had a new success with my niece. To-morrow he will have his money. He is on the crest of the wave. This is the height of the season. In the winter the whole coast is dead. There is an old saying about making hay while the sun shines. Like most of these old sayings there is a good deal of truth in it.'

Again he paused. Neither of them said anything.

'Now the man who planned all this is no fool. This is certain. I told Pinaud here this morning that I will pay the money to-morrow, but he will be there in order to catch the kidnapper. But I am not at all convinced that he will. Not even our Pinaud can achieve the impossible.

'In the first place, I should not think that he will collect the money himself, but will pay someone else to do it. Secondly, the place and the time have been chosen with diabolical cunning. Eleven o'clock on a Saturday morning, in the one Post Office in the town, at the height of the holiday season during a spell of exceptionally fine weather. Imagine the people — all buying stamps for their postcards — drawing their pensions — getting extra money for their holiday expenses — sending off parcels and presents and everything else. The crowd will be fantastic. You can be sure that this is a time and a place chosen for a special reason. That is why I have thought out an alternative plan.'

The girl moved in her chair.

'How will he take Mademoiselle Lahaye to the Golden Lion, m'sieu, as he says in his letter? For all he knows, we may get Inspector Dumont to surround the hotel with his men.'

M. Pinaud thought that her voice was as lovely as her appearance. He also considered it to be an intelligent question.

From the tone of M. le Chef's voice as he replied, he obviously thought that it was nonsense.

'I told you the Post Office was a busy place. Even if we see someone picking up the envelope — which I doubt — it will probably turn out to be a young boy. If we question him he will say that a perfect stranger offered him ten francs to take it to the nearest *café* and wait at an outside table until he collected it. And then I will never see my niece again. I should think there will be a message or a telephone call to where the taxi is waiting, and then he will drive her straight to the promenade, which is a crowded and busy street, drop her there and show her or tell her where to walk and where we shall be waiting for her. Do you agree with me, Pinaud?'

'Yes, m'sieu,' he replied meekly. He did not dare to look at the girl as he spoke. He still thought hers had been an eminently intelligent question, but there was no doubt that the old bastard had answered it with equal intelligence. The only difference was that one had lovely hair and eyes and a body that stirred a fever in his blood and the other had a mind as sharp as a sword and paid his wages. Meekness was in order.

'Good. The main object is to pay the money and get my niece back safely. If you see who takes the envelope, Pinaud, follow him and see what you can do. I will go straight to the Golden Lion and wait there as instructed. If you have no luck, meet me there. Then we come back here and start my plan.'

He looked up suddenly as if expecting some comment, but they both waited silently in dutiful expectation.

'Very few people travel to a holiday resort on a Sunday night. They usually start off with the week-end. But Monday is often a busy day. Sometimes there are things to clear up at home during the week-end.

'And so on Monday night Denise Roche here will take the same train from the *Gare du Nord*, the one that arrives at seven-thirty. She will travel alone and take a small suitcase. I told you my reasons for expecting this to happen again. Personally I am convinced that it will. You, Pinaud, will be waiting and watching the arrival of that train. You have enough experience to find an unobtrusive place, beside other cars whose drivers are doing the same thing. You are going back to-day in an entirely different car, which should be a great help. I organised this in the pool as soon as you had left. Too many people already know the other one.

'Denise will be the first off the train and make for the leading taxi. I think your idea about that first taxi is a good one. You follow it if she gets in. If nothing happens and she is taken to the Golden Lion, have a meal, and then you can take her back to the station. I think there is another train about nine-thirty. Then she will do the same thing again the next day. And the following days, if necessary. Each day until they strike again. The beauty of this plan is that if anything happens, Pinaud, to prevent you from following, we can pay the money to get Denise back and try again with a different operative. I am convinced that we shall not have to wait very long. I will keep my telephone free for you, Pinaud, every night.'

He leaned back in his chair with a self-satisfied smile.

'Right, then — that is that. Any questions?'

Denise Roche held the arms of her chair and stood up.

'No, m'sieu. I am quite ready to go.'

M. Pinaud had been listening with grave attention. Now he stood silently for what seemed like a very long time, without answering the question, his features rigid and sombre with the intensity of his thoughts.

Then at last he spoke, very quietly.

'Yes, M'sieu. I have one or two.'

He looked towards the chair and spoke to the girl.

'Would you be kind enough to wait for me in the office downstairs, Mademoiselle Roche. There are some things I would like to ask you.'

He turned again to M. le Chef and added:

'Naturally — with your permission, m'sieu?'

'Of course. I will see you later, Denise.'

'Thank you, m'sieu.'

She walked to the door with swift and elegant steps and left the room.

★ ★ ★

As the door closed, M. le Chef waved his hand towards the chair.

'You may as well take it, Pinaud.' he said. 'You have never had one before.'

But M. Pinaud shook his head.

'No, thank you, m'sieu. I would prefer to stand.'

M. le Chef looked at him curiously, started to speak, and then changed his mind. He next looked at M. Pinaud thoughtfully for a long moment and then said something quite different in a very quiet voice.

'What is it, Pinaud?'

'I would like to say, m'sieu, that I do not agree with your plan to use this girl as a decoy.'

'Indeed. And why not?'

'Basically it is a good and logical idea — in theory. But not in practice. Not with a girl like this and these people we are dealing with.'

'What do you mean?'

'You have read the letter. You know with what filth you are dealing. This girl may be an operative, but she is also a human being. Use your imagination, m'sieu. Surely it is not worth the risk to send her on a mission like this. To find this kidnapper and his gang is a job for men. These are not men — but animals. That truck must have been driven over Mansard's face several times after he was dead — why? They left the body to be found deliberately and there were identification papers in his pocket. It was probably the driver of that same truck who tried to kill me. And as yet I have done nothing except to make a few enquiries. They will stop at nothing.'

M. le Chef considered for a long moment before he replied. During that time M. Pinaud wondered what had driven him to speak so forcefully and so intensely. With that complete and characteristic self-honesty which was an integral part of his nature he admitted to himself that had Denise Roche been skinny, flat-chested and ugly, his argument might have been presented with less conviction.

'Obviously, Pinaud, there is nothing in what you have said that I can refute. You are completely right. And if you can think of a different plan, tell me, and we will use it at once instead of mine. At the moment, I cannot think of a better one. Let us hope that we achieve something to-morrow at the Post Office. But I doubt it very much.

'And besides, I think you are worrying too much. This kidnapper does not harm his hostages, provided the money is paid. As witness my niece. And I can assure you that we have taken every precaution. Denise Roche will have a new and genuine set of identity papers in her handbag and the established address of a parent here in Paris who will pay for her ransom.'

But still M. Pinaud was not convinced.

'That may be, m'sieu. As I said, it is a

very good plan in theory. But theory is not the same as practice. It is when the unexpected things begin to go wrong — perhaps when she will see or notice something, like Mansard did — something that they do not dare to ignore — that is when she will be in danger. Real danger. And helpless — in the hands of animals.'

Once again M. le Chef looked at him thoughtfully for a long moment.

'You are very eloquent in — '

The interruption came with a violence that matched its speed. The very words seemed to tremble with an intensity of emotion that the listener found shocking to hear.

'So would you be, m'sieu, if you had seen the dead body of Mansard's young daughter in the morgue. I did.'

There was a very long silence. But it was not an uncomfortable one. M. Pinaud had said the words he felt compelled to say, out of the black nightmare that had been under his mind and in his memory ever since he had seen her. He had nothing more to say. M. le

Chef could not find the right words to express his admiration, his esteem and his respect for this man who meant so much more to him than he would ever admit, and therefore he said nothing.

The silence lengthened until in some inexplicable way it seemed to become a communion between them, and until the slow and somehow surging silence healed the agony on the one side and brought compassion and understanding to the other.

'I am sorry,' said M. le Chef quietly.

'You are generous, m'sieu. There is no need to apologise. Perhaps I have too much imagination. She had been sexually assaulted — at her age.'

Again there was a silence. It is a pity that his chronicler was not present at this interview, or he would certainly have mitigated his poetic flights of fancy concerning red-hot lust in sincere admiration for his hero's genuine and commendable concern.

It was M. le Chef who broke it.

'May I say once again that I am sorry, Pinaud — but remember that we both have our duty to do. If we have made no progress by to-morrow my decision to implement this plan of a decoy must stand. It is the only thing we can do. This girl has been specially trained by intensive courses. She knows the risks and has accepted them. There has been no compulsion from anyone.'

M. Pinaud knew when he was beaten. He had tried and failed. There was no point in going on.

'Very well, m'sieu. I will be at the Post Office tomorrow just before eleven o'clock. And I will meet the train at seven-thirty on Monday.'

8

In the office Denise Roche was talking animatedly to a young detective. Or perhaps to put it a little more accurately, she was talking with all her charming animation and he was listening and staring at her, his eyes wide with dog-like devotion.

M. Pinaud interrupted them without the slightest compunction. On the ladder of priority and importance, this one stood with his foot on the bottom rung. But he was in no way to be pitied. Rather, he was to be envied, in that his whole life, to make or to mar, was still before him.

'I am sorry to have kept you waiting,' he said quietly. 'Would you mind coming outside with me?'

'Of course not.'

She turned to the young man.

'Good-bye — thank you so much for listening to me.'

His mouth opened but no sound issued

from it. He was too overcome for speech.

They walked out of the office together, along the corridor and out of the building.

'Where are we going?' she asked.

'To the first *café*. I need a drink — a large one. And I want to talk to you. Do you drink?'

'That depends on what sort of man is paying for it.'

'Do I pass?'

'I think so.'

'Good. Do you like absinthe?'

'Yes. But a small one for me. You heard that I have got to go back to him.'

'Yes. I heard.'

The first *café* was not far. They sat at an outside table in the sunshine, in front of the baskets of flowers and potted shrubs, and the waiter came at once to take their order.

'One special and one small one for Mademoiselle.'

'Yes, m'sieu — right away. Good to see you again.'

'Thank you.'

She smiled at him.

'They know you, then?'

'Yes. I often come here. Not so far to walk.'

'What is a special?'

'An extra large tumbler which holds more absinthe than the largest measure they are legally entitled to sell.'

Now she laughed. Her smile too, he thought as he answered her question, that had been something special. And now she laughed — a happy, carefree and delightful sound.

The waiter appeared beside them. From his tray he took one normal size and one enormous absinthe, a carafe of water and an ice-bowl. All this he did in rotation, with all the flourishes worthy of a favoured client.

M. Pinaud gave him a note and waved him away. He took up the enormous glass swiftly and held it out towards her.

'To you,' he said quietly. 'And to your happiness and safety.'

She looked at him for a long moment, very thoughtfully. She was obviously surprised. This was not what she had expected. Then she raised her own glass and touched his.

'Thank you. That is the most charming, thoughtful and considerate toast I have ever heard. May I repeat it — and to yours.'

'Thank you.'

He drank deeply and set the glass down half empty. Now there was no smile. Perhaps he had imagined the laugh. If he had been able to hear the dead child laugh he was sure it would have been the same.

Now the features opposite him were grave and composed. In them he could see dignity, intelligence and understanding. And that old fool upstairs was going to send her — in spite of all he had said — to end up perhaps on another iron tray in the same morgue.

He snatched up his glass and emptied it in one gigantic swallow. Then he pressed the bell for the waiter.

The girl did not say anything. She just sipped at her glass and watched him. And in her eyes he was sensitive enough to see pity and concern, pain and understanding.

What is the matter with you, Pinaud, he thought with a kind of desperate and savage scorn — you have just met this girl and already you can think of nothing else. Stop behaving like a lunatic. You are a happily married man and the father of children. You have already made for yourself a reputation which you know you can enhance even more successfully. Why have you suddenly gone mad?

Even in the midst of this merciless self-castigation he realised that this girl's understanding silence was something greater than he deserved.

The discerning waiter, having changed the note at the till and weighed his pocket down with the change, had the intelligence and the acumen to answer the bell not with a question but with another enormous glass of absinthe already on his tray. He pocketed another note with barely concealed delight at his own foresight. Who was he to disobey that imperious wave of his client's hand?

M. Pinaud drank some more.

'I needed that,' he said simply.

'Was it — was it something — when

you stayed behind?'

'Yes. How old are you, Mademoiselle Roche?'

'Twenty-two. Would it not be better to make it Denise — if we are going to work together?'

He lifted his glass and drank again. Then suddenly he smiled and she was amazed at the transformation of his hard, strong and brooding features.

'Yes again to the first question. I tried my utmost to persuade him not to use you, but I did not succeed. And no to the second one, Mademoiselle Roche.'

He offered no explanation for his reply to her second question. A faint flush rose to her brow but she did not speak. He took the tongs and dropped a cube of ice into his glass.

'Tell me about yourself,' he said. 'What made you take this kind of work?'

'There is not very much to tell,' she replied without hesitation. 'It is a job that pays reasonably well, and I need the money. My mother is crippled with arthritis, and nursing is expensive. I am young and fit, and they gave me plenty of courses. They seem pleased with what I have done up-to-date. I can take care of myself.'

'Care — rot — nonsense — stupidity. Six courses in unarmed combat — with the physique of a woman? What use is that against a gun or two or three thugs?'

'That is just what they teach you on the course.'

'Madness. You would not have a chance.'

And he drank again, deeply.

'Why are you so concerned, M'sieu Pinaud? Two hours ago you had never heard of me.'

'Because this is not work for a woman. He said that he had told you everything about this case before I came in. Therefore you must have seen the letter — you know what type of man this kidnapper is. You heard what happened to Mansard and his daughter. Supposing we run into something unforseen. What if he has an accident and kills himself to-morrow on the road to Rouplage? Do you think anyone will ever see his niece again?'

He looked at his glass and was surprised to see that it was empty. Now everyone with any experience of it knows that absinthe is a treacherous drink. It lifts you up with fantastic ease, but it lets you down just as far. And there was no doubt that he had not only drunk too much but also drunk it too quickly.

Moodily he pressed the bell again for the waiter. He did not realise with what intensity and emotion he had spoken. It had not been until this afternoon, when he had spoken to M. le Chef, that he had realised how deeply, painfully and tragically this case had affected him.

The girl too, had listened with surprise to what he had just said, not so much to the meaning of the words, but at the passionate sincerity with which he had uttered them.

She sat in silence while the attentive waiter earnt himself another tip, as if thinking what to say in answer. Her glass was not yet empty. Then, once he had gone, she spoke.

'I think it is no use worrying about a thing before it happens. Anyway, I have no choice. I am employed, and I have been given my orders. The only thing for me is to do my best. You can be sure that I will do that.'

He lifted his glass and drank more absinthe. He realised that he was wasting his time. Very few men have ever won an argument with an itelligent, determined and obstinate woman.

'Very well, Mademoiselle Roche,' he said heavily. 'Then there is nothing more to be said. I will be waiting outside the station for the seven-thirty train on Monday. Be sure that you leave your seat in time, so that you can stand by the carriage-door and be the first one out. Then go straight to the first taxi at the head of the line. I will be following you and if everything is all right I will see you in the Golden Lion.'

'That is all quite clear, M'sieu Pinaud. Thank you for your concern for me.'

She lifted her glass to finish her drink. That gave him an excuse to do the same. He stood up and took her back to the *Sûreté* without saying anything more. He said good-bye to her unsmiling, shook her hand politely and went on to the car pool at the back of the building.

He wondered why he had refused to call her Denise. It was a lovely name. She was a lovely girl. But this case meant work — hard and dangerous work, as he knew only too well, and everyone knew that work and pleasure should always be kept separate. At least, that was how he had been brought up, by loving if old-fashioned parents.

Perhaps it had been an instinctive reaction against what he knew was happening to him. He had few illusions about himself. One thing could so easily lead to another. They were two operatives assigned to a murder case, not a newly married couple spending their honeymoon at the Golden Lion. And then he remembered, with guilt and remorse and sadness, that once, not so very long ago, he had thought Germaine to be the only lovely name . . .

But then everyone knows that absinthe is a treacherous drink.

★   ★   ★

He drew another car and drove back to Rouplage in a mood of frustrated despair. As he drove he tried to analyse the reasons for this mood.

In the first place, he had obeyed M. le Chef's instructions, and after he left the car pool had gone straight back to his flat to change his suit. Now at this time in his career M. Pinaud owned only two suits. One was the respectable one he always wore when he was engaged on a case, the other was his really best suit, in which he had once been married, and which he only wore on very special occasions. With the result that since he had undoubtedly put on weight in the last few years, this suit was just a little too tight for a hot summer's day and just uncomfortable enough to be irritating.

He had always meant to have it altered, but somehow he never found the time to take it to the tailor, wait to be measured and call for it to bring it back home.

Secondly, he was more than hungry, he was starving. By the time he had made the two journeys across a considerable portion of the width of the city — for his modest flat was nowhere near the *Sûreté* — and searched the whole place until he finally located it, lovingly folded and wrapped in tissue-paper and mothballs in a large cardboard box at the back of his wife's wardrobe, and changed, his time for lunch had only been long enough for a glass of wine and a sandwich.

What sort of lunch was that for a man with his healthy appetite, he thought morosely as he gave up trying to pull the cutting edge of his waistcoat from out of his armpit and unbuttoned all the five buttons instead.

That was better. It was a pity that he could not do the same thing with his trousers. That discomfort was in a far more vital place.

Now he could have two hands on the wheel and drive much faster. Although there was not much point in doing that. Speed would make him too early again for dinner. He would have to use the same routine as last night. It was a good thing that he had made friends with them all, both in the restaurant and in the kitchen. He remembered that magnificent meal with affection and decided not to stop for a snack on the way, in spite of his hunger, in case he spoilt his appetite.

What sort of a case was this — in which one day he had no time for lunch and the next had to be content with a miserable sandwich?

Which brought him to thirdly. The most important reason of all. What sort of case indeed — in which a young and lovely girl was deliberately being used as bait and exposed to risks that made his blood run cold. What if they suspected and found out? They had no difficulty in finding out what Mansard knew. He should have argued more with the old fool. He should never have accepted defeat so easily. There must have been another way. Why could he not have thought of it?

The unbroken line of giant poplar trees swept by in one continuous blur, as if mocking his thoughts, as if sneering at the futility of all endeavour.

He took his foot off the accelerator, slowed up and pulled in to the side of the road.

Perhaps you have got your braces too tight, Pinaud, he told himself severely. You were in a mad rush when you adjusted them. Then loosen them now. And stop acting like a schoolboy, just because you had three drinks too quickly. Think about your work, your reputation, your career. There. These braces are much more comfortable now. Think about what you have got to do.

He glanced in the rear mirror, let in his clutch and shot off again.

You must not leave this car in the forecourt of the hotel. Nor in a garage. There are three of them, but you do not know which one may be on the payroll. Leave it at the station then. Park it close to the warehouses. Leave it there all night and walk back to the hotel. You have no suitcase, nothing to carry. You should be there in half-an-hour, well before the seven-thirty and the taxis arrive. In that way no-one will notice it, or if they do, know whose it is.

For the rest of the drive he concentrated on thinking about what they would give him for dinner. Whatever it was, he felt quite convinced that it would not be the same as last night. A cook of that quality had too much pride in his work to even think of repetition.

To a hungry man this was quite an interesting speculation, and it did a great deal to counteract his depression engendered by the absinthe.

★   ★   ★

He drove straight into the station forecourt after stopping on the corner to verify if there were people and how many taxis waiting for the next train.

There were only two taxis, no people and not many cars at the back of the forecourt, so he parked his car neatly and unobtrusively between two of the warehouses, locked it and walked out of the forecourt back to the Golden Lion.

There was half-an-hour to wait before he could begin to use the same tactics that had served him so well the night before, so he went into the bar to have a drink. There were a few people inside, but no-one he recognised. He ordered an absinthe, because his own experience and the advice of a friend who was an inveterate drinker had warned him that it was never a wise policy to mix one's drinks. He stared in dismay at the pitiful smallness of the glass, lit a cigarette and felt thankful that he had been able to organise things more sensibly in the *café* where he had taken Denise. No. Correction. Where he had taken Mademoiselle Roche.

Over a quiet drink — or maybe two or three he thought as he emptied this one in two mouthfuls — and half-an-hour's relaxation he had hoped to consider some various alternative plans of action for to-morrow morning in the Post Office, depending on how many and what kind of people would be there.

But all he could think of was dark hair and brown eyes, clear and intelligent, a beautiful face and a lovely and graceful figure . . .

He ordered a second absinthe and looked at his watch impatiently. The sooner he went in to eat the better.

It is a well-known and recognised fact

that alcohol loosens the inhibitions and reveals the true nature of the imbiber. It is therefore hardly surprising to relate that as he sat there, impatiently waiting for the moment when he could put some food into his empty stomach, his thoughts had nothing to do with the Post Office and his duty there on the following day, but consisted of a somewhat confused series of conjectures as to whether the short dark hair would remain tidy and in place on a pillow or whether it was long enough to get dishevelled and what it would be like to kiss that determined and yet full-lipped mouth . . .

At last it was time. He finished his third drink and walked out of the bar, leaving all the other occupants still drinking.

In the empty restaurant he took a simple and perhaps childish pleasure in repeating his most successful tactics of the evening before. He charmed the headwaiter, he sent his special congratulations to the cook, he gave an amusing and lively account of how his important business in Paris had resulted in a gobbled sandwich for lunch and he ordered two bottles of his favourite Swiss wine.

By the time he had eaten *hors d'oeuvres*, trout in almond sauce, cold ham and a salad with the most delicious dressing, peach tart, and had finally made severe inroads once again into that magnificent cheese board, he was feeling very much better.

He thought, very sensibly, that as he had drunk rather too much absinthe that day, it might be a good and wise thing to dilute its astounding tenacity with another bottle of that noble, generous and exhilarating Swiss wine. He was going to bed immediately after this wonderful meal. Another bottle would help him to sleep. He suddenly felt very tired. It was obviously the strain and the mental tension of talking to M. le Chef that must have exhausted him.

He undressed, washed, cleaned his teeth, put on his pyjamas, folded his best suit neatly on a hanger in the wardrobe and went to bed.

His last thought in the few moments before he fell asleep was to admit, with that innate honesty of self-criticism which was so characteristic of him, that perhaps M. le Chef, with all his faults, had nothing to do with his exhaustion. And the mental tension really had quite a different name. A lovely name. Denise Roche.

9

He slept long and heavily, and woke up late. He ate a leisurely breakfast, thinking that it was not worth getting tangled up with Dumont and probably delayed by his investigations concerning the dead truck driver. Besides, he wanted to be inside the Post Office well before eleven o'clock, to go in alone and buy something if necessary, if only to get the feel of the place on his own.

But in the promenade, before he arrived at the Post Office, he met Madoule approaching him.

The gypsy was a truly fearsome sight. His suit had obviously been cut by an expensive tailor, but the cloth was a revolting purple colour, which hardly matched a pink shirt patterned with large brown squares. His shoes were of white buckskin with quite high heels.

He had obviously been drinking too much, even at that early hour. He staggered a little as he forced a way through the pedestrians and holiday-trippers who crowded the pavement, and as he came nearer M. Pinaud noticed that the brown eyes had a peculiar withdrawn and unfocused look, as if what they saw and registered was not being correctly conveyed to his mind.

And yet he recognised M. Pinaud.

'Why — hullo there,' he bawled out. 'Is your veruke better?'

The last thing M. Pinaud wanted was to be drawn into idiotic conversation. It was far more important to get inside the Post Office before the others came and see what the place was like.

'If you would excuse me, M'sieu Madoule,' he said politely. 'I am in a very great hurry to — '

'No-one is in a hurry in Rouplage,' was all the answer he got. 'This is a holiday resort, where people come to relax. And to-day is Saturday, which is my day of rest. I am a busy man. All the week I work at my wood and looking after other people's houses, but Saturday is my holiday.'

'That is a very commendable idea,' M. Pinaud told him, forcing a politeness into his voice that he did not feel. Judging by his appearance, the gypsy could at any moment become aggressive, and when one is on duty, Pinaud, he reminded himself, and has an appointment at eleven o'clock with M. le Chef concerning the important matter of his kidnapped niece, one does not get involved in a street brawl with a drunkard. 'But I have an urgent appointment with — ' he continued.

But he did not have a chance. The gypsy stood squarely in front of him and held up his hand. The moving throng of people, shoppers, idlers and sightseers, parted dutifully and walked along the pavement on either side of them.

'I told you about your veruke, didn't I? We Romanies know other things too — raw onion for a wasp sting, raw potato for a wart and spit for a corn. There — I bet you never heard of any of those before in your life.'

'You are quite right.'

'Nor has your doctor.'

'I should not be at all surprised. Look, M'sieu Madoule — I really must go now — why not come and have a drink with me next Saturday. This one I am busy, but the next one I shall be free. I am staying at the Golden Lion.'

'I know.'

'How do you know?'

The question followed instantaneously, but the brown eyes seemed to turn inwards and become completely blank.

'Everyone knows that,' he muttered vaguely. But M. Pinaud could have sworn that the man regretted his statement.

He saw his opportunity, stepped to one side and through a gap in the crowd and in a moment was lost to sight. As he walked quickly up to the Post Office he wondered whether the gypsy's holiday could have had anything to do with the return of the kidnapped girl on the same day.

* * *

M. le Chef, as so often happened, had been compeletely right.

At eleven o'clock on a fine Saturday morning in the height of the season, the premises of the main and only Post Office in Rouplage were literally jammed tight with a mass of seething people.

Some moved. Some remained stationary, completely oblivious of those who wished to move. Those who moved, or rather who tried to move, were motivated by the perfectly reasonable desire to buy stamps for their holiday postcards, to have their holiday parcels weighed before posting, or to draw out extra money for that same holiday. Some had printed rectangular cards for telephone bills and T.V. licences, for which they required the correct stamps, some merely wished to ask questions and some — these were mainly elderly local residents — had come in on Saturday, as they always did, to draw their weekly old-age pensions. They all joined the queues in front of each window.

Those who did not move stood below the enormous collection of printed notices which covered the remaining two walls — that is to say, the half-wall at the far end beside the group of four telephone-boxes and the two half-walls each side of the entrance and exit doors. The remaining wall, opposite the full-length counter, consisted mainly of windows.

They all stood there, feet firmly planted, completely oblivious of the people trying to pass, and read, with a concentration that might have been committing each word to memory, how to buy stamps every week to pay large quarterly bills, how to select the best and cheapest times in which to make a telephone call, where to buy railway stamps to pay for the summer holiday fare and how to tie the string correctly on their parcels so that it did not become loose and the parcels undone.

The long rectangular table ran almost the whole centre length of that vast room. Every chair in front — and there were many — was drawn up and occupied. People were signing pension-books, writing and addressing holiday cards, sticking on stamps, signing Postal Orders — and doing all the things for which that table had been so thoughtfully provided. Family groups were vociferous around the chairs of the postcard writers, telling them what to say.

M. Pinaud was wearing his best suit, as M. le Chef had suggested, but he did not think that this was enough. So as he came through the entrance doors he had slipped on a pair of tinted spectacles and pulled up a silk scarf to hide his mouth, the most easily recognisable feature of the human face.

Now he began to edge his way gently through the crowd towards the far end of the room. The electric clock on the wall indicated ten minutes to eleven. He had time to walk the whole length of the room once and back before M. le Chef appeared. He would have had plenty of time had he not met Madoule.

Half-way along the length of the table he saw Morelli, bending over an open push-chair and talking first to the young boy in it and then up to his mother at the handle.

He continued without stopping to the

far end of the room. All four telephone-boxes were occupied. Several people were awaiting their turn in front of them. One, with his back turned and fidgeting impatiently, was Correvon.

M. Pinaud eased his way politely and carefully through the crowd around the far end of the table and proceded to make progress back to the entrance and exit doors down the other side.

He remembered his manners automatically and mechanically, because he did not wish to become embroiled with someone like Madoule, but his mind was occupied with something quite different. Why should Correvon, the manager of the Golden Lion, who had his own switchboard in the hotel and obviously his own private telephone in his office — why should he come to a crowded Post Office on a Saturday morning and use a public telephone to make a call?

If he used his authority and questioned the man later, he would almost certainly reply that he came out to post an urgent letter and had suddenly remembered a call he should have made earlier. Should the matter be pursued further, he would gladly give the name and address of some personal friend and say that the number was engaged. And no doubt there would be an express letter in the box, which the Postmaster would have no difficulty in finding.

As Dumont had said, there was no evidence and no proof anywhere in this case. M. Pinaud had the grace to feel guilty. Perhaps he had been too harsh in his judgment.

The clock now indicated two minutes to eleven. He walked a little further towards the doors, so that he could see the end of the table. As he came opposite the push-chair he saw that Morelli was now on one knee beside the child, showing him his tie with its large and ornate tie-pin.

He did not pause. He had to be near the end of the table. The doors were opening and closing now even more rapidly and frequently than before as more and more people continued to come in.

He saw M. le Chef pulling back one of

the entrance doors at precisely eleven o'clock, a sealed envelope in his hand. He laid it down on the end of the table as instructed, next to a family all trying to help choose which postcard to send to grandfather, and then went out.

At that exact moment there was a prolonged and piercing scream of sheer agony, hideous, sudden, unexpected and therefore all the more startling.

The whole thing was beautifully timed.

For a few vital seconds everyone's attention was drawn to the yelling child in the push-chair. The people at the counters turned their backs on the clerks who were serving them. They in turn leaned forward on their high stools to try to see themselves through the barred windows. The stamp buyers, the pension drawers, the patient waiters outside the telephone-boxes with their coins clutched in their hands, the postcard writers and the notice readers — all turned and focused their eyes and their undivided attention on the push-chair and the child giving vent to that hideous scream.

Even M. Pinaud's reaction was normal

and inevitable. Startled, he looked immediately from the table to the push-chair.

When he looked back the sealed envelope had gone.

★ ★ ★

He went straight to the family at the end of the table. Madame, who was obviously the mother, a middle-aged lady with kindly and shrewd features and a pleasant twinkle in her eyes, was seated at the table, a pen in her hand and the postcards all spread out in front of her. The four children, two boys and two girls, of various ages and heights, were clustered around her chair. Their criticisms were vociferous, candid and arrogant with the sublime self-confidence of youth, and as he knew had been going on for some time.

'It is no good sending him a card *gastronomique* — his teeth fell out last time he tried to chew,' said the tallest boy.

'Nor one of the blue sea,' added the smallest girl. 'Last year it was too cold for him to go in.'

'Nor the view from the headland,' chimed in her elder sister. 'The doctor would not let him walk up the path.'

'Nor the boats in the harbour,' added the small boy, determined to have his say. 'He was sick when we took him fishing.'

But Madame their mother had the patience of an angel. As indeed, he thought, all mothers must have. One had only to look at their joyous and confident faces to know that here was a happy and well brought up family.

'You are all quite right,' she told them placidly. 'But you must remember that he is a very old man, and lonely, and he loves you all very greatly. He will be most happy and proud when the postman brings him a card signed by all of you. It is not his fault that he is getting old and not feeling well. So here are four cards that we will put on one side, since you are all quite rightly agreed that they would not be suitable. Now let us try very hard and see if we can find a better one.'

Her words had the desired effect. They had all had their say. They bent over the table, each one eager to have the honour of choosing a suitable card that would make grandfather happy.

M. Pinaud did not waste any time. He addressed Madame very politely. He also smiled at her, having heartily approved of every word she had said. And as every reader knows, M. Pinaud's smile was a very special thing.

'Forgive me, Madame, for listening to what you have just told your children, and for interrupting a conference of such supreme importance — but may I ask you a question?'

'Of course, m'sieu — what is it?'

'A sealed envelope was placed over there on the end of the table a few moments ago — at eleven o'clock — just before the child in the push-chair screamed. Did you happen to see who picked it up?'

She shook her head regretfully.

'No — I am sorry, m'sieu. I cannot help you. I saw the gentleman put it down, but we were so busy arguing about this postcard, as you can see, that I thought nothing of it. I presumed he was just going to get some money out of his pocket-book for stamps to post it. And then that dreadful scream — I am afraid we all looked there at once — and only there. Nowhere else. When it was all over the gentleman had gone and taken his envelope with him. Anyone would have thought the child was being murdered — not just the end of a tie-pin stuck in his finger. Some of these young mothers today — '

Here the twinkle in her eyes became more pronounced and she shrugged eloquently.

'Four gives you a greater sense of proportion.'

'Thank you, Madame, for your courtesy. Yes — it must have been that. I will not interrupt you any more. May I wish you success in your task — and advise you not to spend too much time on it. The sun is shining outside — I am sure all your delightful children would far rather be on the beach than in this Post Office. From your charming words to them just now, which I could not help overhearing, grandfather sounds the kind of person who will not think the picture on the card anything like as important as their names signed on the back and the fact that they all thought of him on their holiday. I wish you all a very happy one.'

He walked back to the Golden Lion in the clear bright sunshine, very slowly and thoughtfully.

The plan had the true simplicity of genius. The young mother would have stoutly denied that her offspring's screams were hideous. She would have maintained with true maternal pride and some justification that they were the perfectly natural sequence of having a bloody great sharp pin stuck into his tender flesh. With the tolerance that every mother inevitably possesses after having created a child, she would have been the first to concede that they were loud and unexpected. Therefore they had served their purpose.

On the other hand, he was forced to admit, it might have been an accident. Perhaps Morelli had only been trying to get the young mother to come to his Casino. He had been showing the snake's head with its ruby eyes to the fascinated child and letting him play with it. The small hand could easily have grabbed the sharp end. If Morelli had nothing to do with it, some other diversion could have been already planned, waiting to be put into execution. With that crowd of people, the envelope could have remained on the table un-noticed for a few moments.

And before he went out he had looked across the room at the telephone-boxes. Correvon was inside one, the receiver held to his ear. From the elevated floor of the box he would have a clear view of the far end of the table.

But as Dumont had said, there was no evidence and no proof.

★ ★ ★

M. le Chef was in the reception lounge of the hotel, sitting in a chair which enabled him to see the entrance doors. He was alone, but looking quite cheerful. M. Pinaud lifted an adjoining chair, sat down beside him and lit a cigarette.

'Not yet,' M. le Chef answered his unspoken question.

'You were quite right, m'sieu,' he said quietly. 'With that crowd I could not see who took the money. There was a diversion, either accidental or deliberate, as soon as you had gone. A child suddenly yelled with pain and everyone looked to see why.'

Briefly, factually, he told him what had happened. M. le Chef listened attentively, but never took his eyes from the doors. When M. Pinaud had finished, he nodded his head in agreement.

'I thought it would be something like that,' he said. 'From the choosing of the place and time. These people must obviously be very highly organised. And I have not been here long. I do not expect her yet. The driver of the taxi or car would not dare to come into this forecourt, but will probably take her to the promenade in the middle of a crowd and tell her to walk here.'

As he finished speaking, one of the double doors opened slowly and he sprang to his feet.

'Here she is,' he said, and hastened to meet the young girl who had just come

185

in. He took her small suitcase in one hand and her arm in the other and led her to his chair, where he introduced M. Pinaud who was already on his feet.

He shook her hand with interest. She was small and slender, with fair hair and grey eyes, and as befitted a niece of M. le Chef, looked a well-born lady. She was wearing the same clothes that had been detailed, now somewhat creased and crumpled, and he had no difficulty in recognising her from the photograph.

Just now the grey eyes were strained and dull, her features white, and he noticed that she swayed as she walked.

'It is good to see you safe, Mademoiselle Lahaye,' he told her. 'Please take my chair.'

'This calls for a celebration,' said M. le Chef. 'You look as though you need a brandy, Marie, while you tell us all about it. Let us find a corner in the bar.'

But she held up her hand and made what M. Pinaud could see was a very brave effort to smile.

'You two go and start,' she said. 'I can do nothing until I have had a hot bath — not even talk.'

'Of course,' he agreed quickly. 'I should have thought of that. I will organise it for you at once.'

'Let me, m'sieu,' M. Pinaud told him. 'They know me here. I am an important man — since I received your official envelope from the *Sûreté*.'

He went to talk to his friend Clarisse, earnestly and eloquently, with the result that in an incredibly short time a rosy-cheeked chambermaid came smiling down the stairs, followed the direction of his finger pointing to Marie Lahaye, gave her a strong arm in support and took her upstairs to a bathroom.

The two men went into the bar-lounge, which was not very full at that time. There was one man reading a newspaper, a young couple talking animatedly on the bar-stools and a family party around the centre table. They chose a small table by the window in the corner of the room and M. le Chef went to the bar. He returned with an open bottle of brandy and three glasses.

'Thank you, m'sieu,' said M. Pinaud as

he lifted his glass. 'As you said, this calls for a celebration. I drink to this happy day for both of you.'

'Thank you.'

They drank. It was excellent brandy.

'But,' M. Pinaud continued, 'she does not look well, your niece. It must have been an ordeal. She has courage, that one.'

'Yes. Obviously she will not wish to stay in this place now. I will take her back home with me and then to my doctor, to hear what he advises. Then we can make other plans.'

'Yes. That is wise. It will be interesting to hear what she has to tell us.'

M. le Chef finished his brandy, reached for the bottle, refilled his glass and held it poised in his hand, waiting. M. Pinaud, inspired by such a noble example, obviously did the same and watched the uninterrupted pouring with a dignified approval.

'Interesting — yes,' agreed M. le Chef. 'But I do not for one moment think helpful to us. This operation has obviously been meticulously and cleverly planned, and just as obviously has been carried out many times before. But there is no proof and no evidence. I still think that we shall have to rely on my plan.'

They went on to discuss the case, in all its aspects, over and over again.

There was less than a quarter of the brandy left in the bottle when Marie re-appeared, a clear indication that they had not been wasting their time.

They both stood up and gave her the most comfortable chair. M. le Chef poured her a drink, emptied what was left in the bottle into their two glasses and then waved it cheerfully at the barman.

'This will do you good, my dear,' he told her. 'Now you can relax and tell us all about it.'

'Thank you,' she said as she lifted her glass. 'You are usually right where drink is concerned. I am sorry to have kept you both waiting so long, but the joy and the peace and the luxury of that hot bath was the only thing I could think about for the past two days. It was a dream come true. I could not hurry.'

'Naturally enough,' said M. Pinaud,

watching her drink with a benign approval. 'Already you are looking a different person.'

He lifted his own glass in salutation.

'Your very good health, Mademoiselle Lahaye,' he said courteously. 'And to the happiness of this day of your safe return.'

'Thank you. I felt very bad when I got here, but I am better now.'

He marvelled, as he always did in the presence of women, what miracles could be achieved by the judicious use of a comb, powder, lipstick and rouge.

She finished her drink. M. le Chef promptly re-filled it from the bottle the barman had broken all records in replacing.

'There is not very much to tell,' she said. 'And I am afraid that what there is will not be a great deal of use to you. I was very quickly off the train and went to the first taxi in the queue.'

'What did he look like?' asked M. le Chef. 'Do you remember?'

'No. Who looks at a taxi-driver's face? I just told him the Golden Lion and got in.

I do not think he even turned his head. Even if he had — I would not have seen much. I seem to remember that he wore tinted glasses and had a silk scarf pulled up high.

'He drove from the station to what I think was the promenade — there were still quite a number of people walking about. Then he turned off into a quiet and completely deserted side street and stopped. He left the engine running. He got out and opened the back door very quickly — almost all in one movement — and pressed a cloth over my mouth and nose. It was all so quick and sudden — and so completely unexpected — that it was all over before I even had time to speak, let alone shout or scream. There was a kind of sweet and sickly smell and I heard very faintly the two doors slamming shut before we started off again. Then I did not remember anything more until I woke up — I should think it was the next morning.'

'How did you know that, Mademoiselle?' M. Pinaud asked her. 'Where were you?'

She smiled at him and took another sip from her glass.

'I am coming to that. I was in a tiny little room, like a cupboard. It was not much larger than the small iron bed-frame on which I was lying, and the same rectangular shape. There was a mattress and blankets on the frame. The walls were covered with a plain dark paper. On one of the narrow ends there were joins in this paper, where an oblong panel could be lifted out. There were no doors or handles, just four small holes — I should think they were air-vents — in each top corner.

'It was of course completely dark. I only saw all this in the morning when the panel was lifted out and a man came in. He wore overalls and had a black stocking mask that covered his head completely. He blindfolded me and led me outside. That was when I knew it was morning and that I must have slept — I could smell the fresh air and feel the sun. Then he took me back and told me I could remove the blindfold. He was the one who brought me two meals a day. The food was quite good, but I think there must have been some drug in it, because I felt awful and was quite content to spend all the time just lying on the bed-frame and sleeping.

'Oh — and that first morning he came in again with a pen and paper. He asked me for my name and the name and address of whoever would be prepared to pay money quickly to have me returned safely and unharmed. I gave your name, Uncle, as I thought you could cope rather more efficiently than father, who would only have panicked. He will pay you back, of course.'

'You did the right thing, my dear,' M. le Chef told her. 'I have rather more facilities for organising such a thing.'

'And then what happened this morning?' M. Pinaud asked her.

'I should think they put an overdose of whatever it was in the food. I felt more than awful. I could hardly walk. The man with the mask blindfolded me, led me to the taxi and made me sit in the front. I knew I was beside the driver — I could hear the engine.

'Then after a little while we stopped, the driver got out, opened my door and put me in the back. We started off again and he told me through the partition to take off the cloth from my eyes and pass it through to him.'

'Could you recognise where you were?' M. Pinaud asked her.

She shook her head.

'I have never been here before. It was another quiet side-street which took us at right angles into the main promenade here. He stopped the taxi, came round to the back to open the door and told me which way to walk to the hotel.'

'Was it the same man?'

'I should think so. He had the same tinted glasses and silk scarf. He only pointed and said a few words: Golden Lion — right-hand side — not far.'

'Did you get his number?' asked M. le Chef.

'No — I never even thought of that. I was feeling so awful all the time I could hardly stand — just as if I had a severe *migraine*. I am sorry'

M. Pinaud smiled at her.

'It does not matter,' he said. 'In a different suit and without his glasses and scarf, he would swear that he had never seen you before in his life.'

She seemed pleased at the sympathy and the warm and gentle kindness in his voice.

'Do you really think so? I feel so stupid and so — so guilty at not being able to tell you more.'

'Nonsense,' said M. le Chef cheerfully. 'All this has obviously been done before — they took every precaution to ensure that you would have nothing to tell. Now then — this is supposed to be a celebration in honour of the fact that you are back with us safe and sound. Let us do something about it. What is the food like here, Pinaud?'

'Magnificent. The cook is an artist.'

'All the better. You will join us, of course?'

But M. Pinaud shook his head.

'Not if you will excuse me, m'sieu. You two surely have enough to talk about without having a third at the table.'

M. le Chef looked at him thoughtfully

and appraisingly for a long moment before he spoke.

'Where will you be going then?'

'To Dumont, m'sieu — to see if he has found out anything about that truck-driver.

M. le Chef looked at his watch.

'Then you will find him out now at lunch,' he said. 'To this Inspector lunch is a very important thing. I ought to know — I wasted enough time trying to get him on the telephone from Paris. You come with us. We shall be glad of your company, and afterwards you can go on to Dumont and I will drive Marie home.'

He eyed the fresh bottle on the table with a dignified approval.

'Besides — we already have the brandy to go with the coffee. You know very well we two could never finish that ourselves. I told you it was a celebration.'

'You are very kind, m'sieu,' he said quietly.

Which was hardly what he wanted to say, but he remembered in time that it is a wise detective who does not argue with his employer.

10

'Ah — M'sieu Pinaud — come in — come inside. I have been expecting to see you ever since you telephoned.'

The sonorous and majestic voice had not changed, he reflected as he went into Inspector Dumont's office and sat down in the chair on the opposite side of the desk.

'Thank you,' he said. 'There were two reasons. One that I had to report to Paris, and two that I knew your task would not be an easy one. Therefore the more time I could give you the better.'

Dumont sat down.

'You are quite right, M'sieu Pinaud — completely right. I have had every man available on the job, from the moment we got the truck and the body back here. But so far without any success.'

'What do you mean?'

'I mean that we have compiled some small information — none of which is going to help us in any way.'

'And what is that?'

Dumont opened the file on his desk and began to read.

'Name Marc Lebrun. Age forty-two. Gave his occupation as independent builders' assistant. He kept no accounts, paid no tax, had no family and lived alone in one of those cheap municipal cottages in the Rue Bernard, behind the station. He would use the truck, which he had bought second-hand for cash, for any odd job, provided he was paid in the same way. He used to leave it outside in all weathers, since there are no garages to the cottages and the Rue Bernard is nothing more than a lane. Apparently, according to his neighbours, he was a heavy, surly and solitary drinker and a man of bad reputation who would do anything provided he got paid for it.'

Dumont looked up from the file.

'Just the type to be used by a kidnapper who did not wish to soil his hands, you would agree, M'sieu Pinaud?'

'Of course. He did not try to kill me or put me out of action for nothing. I was expecting something like this — that is why I asked you to investigate. Did your men find out from anyone whether he had been seen in the Golden Lion or the Casino?'

Dumont shook his head.

'No. He was a man who kept very much to himself. No-one seems to know which builders gave him work or even what he carried in his truck. Our two local firms both deny ever having employed him. His neighbours are all poor, but honest and respectable types. Actually, one of my men learnt more about him from the proprietor of the local café than from any of them.'

He looked down again at the file.

'But perhaps your last question can be answered in another way, M'sieu Pinaud.'

'What do you mean?'

'In these small and simple cottages, erected by the town council with municipal and state funds for those who cannot afford to pay rent, Lebrun was the only occupant with a brand-new telephone. His tale was that its installation was essential for his haulage business.'

He closed the file.

'I think I might not have been so far wrong with my two suspects. There would have been no need for him to make himself conspicuous by going to the Golden Lion or the Casino. He only had to pick up the telephone for his instructions.

'I would have put a tap on it,' M. Pinaud told him.

The majestic voice soared at least three notes higher in righteous indignation.

'How could I? I did not even know the man existed until — '

'Until I killed him. I realise that. I have no regrets. He tried to kill me first. But when these kidnappings started I would have put that on my standing orders to the telephone company for all new installations.'

'But there was no proof — '

'Suspicious circumstances — quite enough.'

'I doubt if it would have done any good,' Dumont said. 'If any messages were telephoned to him, you can be sure that they apparently concerned only building materials and sounded perfectly harmless. But they would have meant something quite different to him.'

'That may be. But it would have been worth trying. Anyway, it is too late now.'

'Yes. We shall get no clues from him now. The man is dead.'

'M'sieu le Chef received the same two letters that were sent to Mansard,' M. Pinaud told him. 'They were delivered by special service. He paid the ransom in the Post Office this morning, and his niece is now with him.'

'Good. I could have lent you some men. They might have seen who took the money — '

'We thought of that.' M. Pinaud interrupted, 'but he did not dare to risk it. In a town like this your men are all probably known by sight, if not by name.'

He told Dumont what had happened in the Post Office, but he did not mention anything about Denise Roche. And he told him how he had called at all the houses on the headland immediately after Lebrun had tried to put him out of action and how he had even searched Madoule's cottage, but without success.

'Both Correvon and Morelli, your two suspects, have resident housekeepers and staff in their houses,' he continued, 'because they do a good deal of entertaining. It is hardly likely that either of them would be able to keep a kidnapped girl under the same roof. That would mean telling far too many people and spending all the profit in buying their silence. That does not mean that either one or both are not suspect. My theory is that Lebrun was paid to drive the bodies to the headland so that they could be discovered quickly by one of the early morning tradesmen. They and Marie Lahaye may well have been taken from the station to a house or a flat in quite a different part of the town.'

'And now — without Lebrun — we shall never know,' said Dumont.

M. Pinaud looked at him very thoughtfully for a long moment before he replied.

'I do not agree with you, Inspector Dumont,' he said quietly. 'I shall know. I am making it my business to know. That is why I am here.'

He stood up from his chair.

'I will keep in touch,' he said as he turned to go. 'Let me know at the hotel if you find out anything new.'

'You can count on me, M'sieu Pinaud. Two of my men are still on the job. They will continue.'

'Good. And thank you.'

He went out, left the police-station and walked back slowly to the hotel, thinking deeply. Why did you make no mention of M. le Chef's plan, Pinaud, when you were in Dumont's office, he asked himself. If you two are supposed to be working together, surely he is entitled to know. Otherwise, how can he help? M. le Chef is so proud of his plan he would have expected you to tell him. The Inspector might have been able to do something — to guard against some unforseen contingency. After all, he has the men and the organisation.

Be honest with yourself. That, with all your faults, you have always been. Is it because you do not want him interfering, thereby alerting these unscrupulous and merciless people and perhaps endangering her life? You know you have no confidence in him. You know that he was investigating the Mansard case before you were sent here, and in charge of how many others before, which he airily dismissed as solved because he never heard anything more about them.

You saw that small dead face in the morgue, Pinaud. That is something you will never forget. How many others came to the same or an even more horrifying end because their parents could not find the money for the ransom? Or because he told them confidently that the missing girl had met a boy-friend on the train and gone to a different hotel and to just wait until she came to her senses?

You do not know. Since you are being honest with yourself you are bound to admit that you do not know.

He had come to the hotel. He had a few drinks in the bar, another excellent meal in the restaurant and went to bed early. It had been an exhausting day.

★　★　★

The next day was Sunday. There were many things he could have done, but from his considerable experience he was quite confident that the unsolved cases of the Mansard murders and the Rouplage kidnappings were unlikely to make much progress towards any solutions. There were too many other things to be done on a Sunday. For that it had been provided.

What he actually did was typical of the man.

He walked, quickly and unobtrusively, down the busy promenade to the railway station to get his car. A train had just arrived, so he spent a few moments in an intense and absorbed study of the large printed timetables on the wall of the entrance-hall. This exercise in absorbed concentration continued until the last three taxis in the queue had driven off empty to try their luck elsewhere and the only private cars in the forecourt were the ones parked in orderly lines for the day.

He eventually walked to get his car from the side of the warehouse in that deserted and somnolent hush which inevitably seems to envelop all provincial and country stations between the arrival and departure of trains. He was reasonably certain that no-one saw him get in, start up and drive away.

He drove, quietly and carefully on indirect gear, through the busy town. Then he drove for nearly four hundred kilometres very fast, easy and relaxed, his packet of cigarettes open on top of his lighter on the empty seat beside him, his mind deliberately denying all thought save the supreme concentration of driving. M. le Chef, magnanimously basking in the reflected glory of his master plan, had been gracious enough to give him a better, larger and even faster car.

He rejoined the main N1 outside the town and kept on it as far as Beauvais, where he took the N181 out to join the N70 at Chartres. There he parked the car in front of the Cathedral and got out to stretch his legs. The morning sun was making a wonder of the great circular rose window and he stood for a long and reverent moment, bare-headed, lost in awe and admiration at the majesty and the ineffable beauty of all that glory of tinted glass and delicately traceried stone.

As he walked back to the car he had the strange and yet convincing certitude that he had also been inside to worship . . .

* * *

Before Poitiers he left the main road and followed the signpost to Morillon, the village outside which Germaine's parents lived on their small farm. At the bridge he turned up the lane, past the church and the cemetery until he eventually reached the old farmhouse, the out-buildings and the barns, and in spite of the joyous and penetrating shouts of his children he yet managed to hear the love and the anxiety in his wife's voice as she reproached him — quietly and yet with heartfelt thankfulness — for driving so far on what should have been his day of rest.

It was indeed his day of rest, he thought swiftly and thankfully as he was taken, happily and vociferously, across the lawn that the fierce gander and his family kept perpetually neat and tidy to the first field where the new foal leaned his dainty legs, long out of all proportion, for support against his mother's side and the two nuzzling calves opened their calm and liquid eyes even wider in mild astonishment at the noise.

Then across the yard with the baby chickens in their hen-coop to the barn with the enormous sow suckling her tiny pink piglets on the straw of her sty, and the kittens in the hay on a shelf beside them.

Even as the children held his hands and laughed and chattered and showed him everything that was so new and so exciting in comparison to their daily lives in a city flat he reflected again — with the strange and vivid wonder of inconsequential thought — how true it should be that this was indeed his day of rest.

He had never been able to afford hotel bills for a summer holiday for three. There had always been too many things to buy with an inadequate salary. Their washing-machine had disintegrated, hardly surprisingly, a few years after the children's infancy. The money he had been compelled to save to buy a new one might well have paid a hotel bill at Rouplage, amongst all those prosperous types he had encountered on the promenade, so that his own children could have climbed ecstatically all over the fishing-boats in the harbour and made castles on the sandy beach of the foreshore.

The thoughts of Rouplage brought back memories — stark and sudden and tragic — of the morgue, the small slain body and the dead pale face . . .

And in the bright hot sunshine of that lovely summer's morning he sensed the scintillations at the corners of his sight and he saw the blank yellow opaqueness surge up in front of his eyes to cloud and obscure his vision, and in desperation he clutched his daughters' hands even more tightly to counteract and nullify the physical onslaught of the *migraine* engendered so suddenly and so typically by the tension of his thoughts and the intensity of his over-vivid imagination . . .

If he had been able to afford a holiday

in Rouplage as well as a new washing-machine — if he had tried to find out, as Mansard had tried, as he himself would obviously have tried, to find some clue to put an end to this whole filthy business — then he might well have been a father in that morgue, looking down in horror at what was left of his daughter . . .

There, but for the grace of God, he thought solemnly — and then started guiltily at the sudden unexpectedness of a childish and accusing voice:

'Daddy — stop — stop — you are hurting me — you are squeezing my hand — '

He said he was very very sorry and knelt to kiss the part he had hurt, and promised that he would never do such a thing again.

Later, as they sat in the stone-flagged kitchen of the farmhouse, eating bread and cheese and drinking home-brewed cider, the *migraine* passed, as it always did, leaving its inevitable aftermath of doubt, apprehension, incredulity and dismay . . .

But the memories remained, like

searing knives on an open wound — as he knew they would always remain. What if it had been his own daughter?

★　★　★

The time passed all too quickly.

He had another good and fast run back and arrived at Rouplage in the evening physically exhausted but mentally at peace.

The fine weather broke as he neared the coast, and wind, cloud and rain came in with the late tide. He switched on the windscreen wipers and drove straight to the station, where he parked the car beside the same warehouse and walked philosophically back through the driving rain to the hotel.

There he thoroughly enjoyed another gigantic meal, somewhat later than had been his habit, complimented the cook with his usual enthusiasm, and then went to bed exceptionally early, where he slept like a child for twelve hours.

★　★　★

By the time he had finished his breakfast he realised that lunch would be served very shortly. He therefore gave serious consideration over a modest drink as to what decision he ought to make, bearing in mind the importance of the problem, and came to the logical conclusion that what he had been about to do could not possibly be affected in any way by doing it after he had eaten.

He had missed his normal Sunday mid-day meal yesterday. To a man with his healthy appetite this was not a memory to be lightly forgotten. He remembered without regret. The bread and cheese in the kitchen had been inevitable, in order that he could have more time to spend with his family. But there was no need to be foolish and to make a habit of such nonsense, especially since M. le Chef was paying the hotel-bill. Petrol to Morillon on his expense-sheet might well have been a debatable — even an acrimonious point in the opinion of M. le Chef, but there could be no argument about a hotel-bill incurred in the implementation of his own master plan.

He sighed with satisfaction as he stood up from the bar-stool and made his way back to the restaurant. His thinking, as always, had been completely and profoundly logical.

After thoroughly enjoying another of those excellent meals he had come to expect, he left his table, put on his raincoat and walked out into the driving rain.

He had no difficulty in finding the *café* in the small street at the end of the Rue Bernard. It was the only one. At that hour it was deserted. The proprietor was a small and sallow Italian, with a protuberant stomach contained with difficulty by a tightly tied and not too clean apron, and bright, suspicious and beady black eyes.

Hardly the type, M. Pinaud essayed a shrewd guess as he sat down at a corner table, with whom Dumont's detectives would have had a marked success. No blame to them. No fault of theirs. Dumont was the type who would make a big fuss over an expense-sheet.

But this was different. This was the

Sûreté itself investigating, in the person of Pinaud, its most celebrated detective. This called for absinthe, which no local detective in a seaside resort would ever dare to claim as an expense. Absinthe was known to be a treacherous drink, and yet even its detractors were compelled to admit a remarkably successful one.

He ordered a bottle, asked for two glasses, a carafe of iced water and invited the proprietor politely to join him at the table.

In a daze of profound astonishment mingled with unconcealed delight, the little man hastened to comply. Whoever this one might be, he certainly did not come from the municipal cottages in the Rue Bernard. This one must be from the big city. This one was not only of an extreme generosity, but obviously of the greatest importance.

He watched the milky-white opaqueness swirling up to meet the ice-cubes with awe, wonder and fascination as M. Pinaud poured, gratified to learn that his shrewd assumption of human nature was not only correct but confirmed as he was informed that he was drinking with Auguste Mischoud, a lawyer who could afford an office in the Boulevard Haussmann.

It was a simple matter of the late Jean Lebrun, M. Pinaud continued to lie cheerfully and willingly, and a small legacy which might possibly be proved to be of interest to his heirs or dependants.

But not even the absinthe could enable the proprietor to make bricks without straw. With the best will in the world, he could add very little to what Dumont had already said.

'A lonely man, M'sieu Mischoud,' the man said, lifting his glass with an obvious regret that its contents seemed unable to inspire him to greater flights of eloquence. 'A man who lived alone. No family. A morose individual. An introverted type. Mind you — you have come to the right place here. You did well by coming to see me. If there was anything to tell, I would be the man to tell you. But there is not.'

He shook his head despondently, sighed mournfully and emptied his glass regretfully. M. Pinaud promptly refilled it.

'Thank you. Thank you very much, m'sieu. He seemed to have very few friends, but always plenty of money. No-one knew how he earned it. He used to come in here to spend it on drink, which he could not hold. He became surly and quarrelsome. Sometimes that gypsy type Madoule would drink with him — the one who lives in the old cottage on the headland. He too, had plenty of money, but a better and stronger head. They made a fine couple.'

M. Pinaud sighed philosophically as he drank. At least it was good absinthe.

'Ah well,' he said. 'No harm done. I shall have to get the police to make routine enquiries. I thought you might have had some information which would have saved time.'

'I am sorry, m'sieu,' said the proprietor, eyeing the bottle with a wistful regret.

'Never mind,' M. Pinaud told him cheerfully. 'They may get more information from his neighbours.'

He lifted the bottle and looked at it thoughtfully.

'Well,' he continued with all the conviction of one who knows that he is undoubtedly right, 'There is not much point in keeping this small amount, is there? Drink up, m'sieu — and then I must go.'

The proprietor watched him in speechless and fascinated awe and then bowed him out of the *café* with something that was not far short of reverence

11

M. Pinaud chose his time judiciously. A good few moments before the seven-thirty train was due in, he drove his car slowly and quietly from the warehouse to the station forecourt, where he parked it neatly in line with the other cars there for the same purpose.

At an angle from the main entrance, he had a good view of the inner line of waiting taxis and would have an unobstructed run to the exit road. The weather had changed again with the evening tide; the rain had ceased, the sun was trying to pierce the clouds but the wind was still high. He lit a cigarette and settled down to wait.

He noticed that the driver of the taxi at the head of the waiting queue was wearing tinted glasses and a silk scarf, and was leafing through the pages of an illustrated magazine. He remembered what Marie Lahaye had told them in the hotel and felt his pulses quicken and his muscles tighten in anticipation. He also remembered every word of sound commonsense that her uncle had uttered in his office. These people, whoever they were, had been successful and now were riding high. It could be that they were confident enough to try again.

The arrival bell changed raucously from the signal-box and the level-crossing gates began to close. The train glided in slowly with a hissing of brakes and a muted throbbing from the diesel-electric motors. The astonishing reverberations of the porter's stentorian voice could be clearly heard in the forecourt; 'Rouplage — Rouplage — end of the line — Rouplage — all change here.'

And then two things happened very quickly. The driver of the leading taxi laid down his magazine and started his engine and Denise Roche, carrying a small suitcase, came out from the entrance-hall of the station.

Good girl, thought M. Pinaud swiftly as he confirmed that the number of the taxi was the one that he had already memorised and started his own engine. She did what I told her. She must have been the first one off the train.

The taxi-driver had put back his arm and hand to open the back door. It slammed shut and the taxi shot away in a burst of astonishing speed towards the exit road which led into the town.

M. Pinaud followed. Or at least he tried to follow. Within seconds his foot was jamming the accelerator hard down on to the floorboard.

His car was both powerful and fast. No ordinary Renault, Citroën nor Peugeot taxi would ever have left him behind with such acceleration. It might have had a taxi body, he thought as he drove like a man possessed to keep up, but to give such a performance must have been fitted with an Italian racing engine under the bonnet.

This was one of the unforseen contingencies for which the master plan had not allowed. This was one of those unexpected things, as yet unknown and undefined, which had given him such a premonition of disaster.

But he could not give up. He could not lose that taxi in front. He had to know where she was being taken — for her sake, for his own sake, for the sake of those who were dead . . .

He knew that he was taking chances. He realised that — on a road which until recently had been soaking wet — he was driving like a maniac. And yet he had to do it.

By superb skill and years of driving experience he narrowed the gap between them just before they came to the beginning of the promenade.

And then, suddenly and unexpectedly, it happened.

A large and gaily striped rubber ball bounced out from the pavement into the road. In almost the same second a small boy ran out right in front of his car to retrieve it.

M. Pinaud's reflexes and muscular co-ordination were immediate, but even as he braked frenziedly he knew — with that blinding clarity which gives the instantaneous wonder to thought — that he could not possibly stop in his own length.

So he took the only available alternative. In the same fractional second that he braked — with practically the same movement — he wrenched the wheel over to the left and drove his car hard into the side of a large single-decker country bus which had been approaching and was now occupying the other half of the road.

The taxi had disappeared. Denise Roche was inside it. In the few moments that followed he could think of nothing else.

The bus had stopped, blocking one half of the road. His own wrecked car, at an angle, blocked the other. Impatient motorists began to hoot. He unclipped his safety-belt slowly and got out.

The driver of the bus, a tall and soldierly figure with a mane of long white hair, slammed his door shut, walked around the front of his bus and strode to meet him with his hand outstretched.

'M'sieu,' he bellowed in a parade-ground voice, 'Whoever you are — that was the most magnificent piece of driving

I have ever seen in forty years behind the wheel. I would be both proud and privileged to shake your hand.'

They did so. Some motorists continued to hoot. They both ignored them.

'Thank you,' began M. Pinaud. 'Anyone would have — '

'No — no — a thousand *sacré* nos. Very few would even have had the guts to try. Fewer still — judging by what I follow on the main roads to-day — would ever have achieved it. You saved that child's life. Where the hell is the young idiot? Decent God-fearing parents would have brought him up at least to say thank you.'

'It has not done my car much good,' said M. Pinaud, feeling embarrassed enough at this praise to change the subject and therefore looking ruefully at what had once been the pride of M. le Chef's car-pool. 'Your bus, m'sieu, was rather more strongly made.'

'Nonsense. Tripe. Cock. Rot. Balderdash. A car can always be repaired. No-one yet has found out how to repair a dead body. Ah — here is the mother to thank you. I will shift my bus to the

National Garage up there — it is only the side panels — and get Voisin to send his tow-car for you. I know him well. Then perhaps you would be kind enough to give me a few particulars — for my company'.

'Of course.'

'Oh, m'sieu — what can I say — how can I ever begin to thank you — '

She had one arm around the shoulders of a somewhat crestfallen small boy. He held the striped ball, for which he had risked so much, tucked firmly under one arm. She had a lovely smile, a beautiful face, and a figure so young, so boyish and yet so sweetly graceful that it seemed more than likely that she must have conceived while still at school.

He wondered swiftly if this was one of the young mothers Dumont had mentioned, staying at a different hotel without a husband but with the custody of a child pending divorce proceedings. It could well be. He did not know what to say. He tried something and felt foolish.

'It was nothing, madame — I had to avoid him. A magnificent ball like that is a precious thing — '

'Oh no — I have warned him — I have told him a hundred — a thousand times. But in obstinacy he resembles his father — '

The bus had gone. An intelligent policeman had appeared and was filtering the traffic alternatively around M. Pinaud's car with considerable competence. The various morons driving, having expressed their indignation by hooting, now drove off decorously. One does not hoot at a policeman.

'But this is hardly the place to talk, m'sieu,' she continued. 'I am staying alone here at the Golden Lion. Room number eight. Would you please come up later — when I have put Etienne here to bed — and allow me to thank you properly. As you fully deserve to be thanked for what you did.'

He shook his head, regretfully but with determination, as he glanced at the rings on her hand.

'You are very kind, madame — but I am afraid I shall have too much to do. As you see, I must wait here for my car to be removed and then hire another one. And then I have work to do after — I am so sorry. But really there is no need — I only did what anyone would have done — '

'Yes — but you did it so well.'

Still he shook his head. She saw that he would not change his mind. And then he watched them go. She looked so crest-fallen and disappointed that momentarily it gave the illusion of being difficult to tell which one was the child. It was a pity she was so lovely, so enticing, so grateful . . .

It might have been an interesting experience to be properly thanked by her.

★ ★ ★

The tow-truck, painted a bright crimson with *Garage Nationale* in gigantic white letters on its sides, arrived quickly. Its driver stopped well in time, waited patiently for a signal from the competent policeman, turned into an alley that separated two blocks of shops, and then reversed slowly and skilfully until the truck was immediately behind M. Pinaud's car.

The driver, a young man with sandy hair and freckles in an immaculate white coat, opened the door and was outside as soon as it had stopped. In his gloved hands he carried a square of towelling. He walked to the back of the truck, loosened two securing nuts in the base of the hoist, pulled down the arm, dropped the towel on the road in exactly the right place, knelt and then lay on his stomach on the tarmac and in a moment the grapnel of the hoist was locked around the back axle of Pinaud's car.

Then he tossed the towel into the open back, walked around to the driving-seat, started the engine and engaged the lifting gear. The hoist-arm moved, vibrated with the strain, and then lifted with the increased power until the whole back of the car came up and the front dipped gently, dropping splinters of broken glass and pieces of mangled metal on to the road.

M. Pinaud and the policeman both converged towards the driving cab. The window was open.

'Thank you for coming so quickly,' said

M. Pinaud gratefully, since he had arrived first.

The young man smiled.

'Simon Voisin, at your service, m'sieu. This is my job. Hop in the other side. Just up the road.'

He did so. Now it was the policeman's turn.

'And what about this mess in the road?'

He asked the question politely and quietly, as befitted a reasonable request. Competence, thought M. Pinaud, has no need for arrogance or bluster.

'Chap on his way now, with a hand-cart. Biggest mess first, father always told me.'

The policeman smiled.

'Quite right. He would. Tell him I will wait beside it. Off you go.'

The young man let in his clutch and drove off, slowly and carefully.

'Two things, M'sieu Voisin,' said M. Pinaud. 'Since you have been good enough to do all this for me, would you care to estimate for the repairs?'

'Very pleased to have the work. Take a couple of days — telephoning for spare parts and all that. We are very busy.'

'That is all right. There is no hurry. The other one is — have you got a car I can hire for about a day or two? I must have one right away.'

'You had better see father for that. I think everything is out except a small Citroën — this is the height of the season.'

They turned into the forecourt of the garage, half of which was already occupied by the bus.

Voisin senior was an older but exact duplicate of his son, even down to another immaculate white coat. He was talking to the bus-driver, but came to meet M. Pinaud as soon as he got out, looked at his card and credentials with interest, but shook his head regretfully when asked for a hire car.

'Only a baby Citroën, M'sieu Pinaud,' he said. 'Too small — which explains why it is still here.'

'Nothing larger or faster? I may have to drive to Paris to-night in a hurry.'

'I am sorry. Everything else is out.'

'What are you buggering about for,

229

René?' boomed the parade-ground voice of the bus-driver as he marched over towards them. 'I just told you what happened. This one is a good type and a driver beyond compare. Take your finger out and help him. He is in a mess through no fault of his own, but because of an idiot child and a moron mother who should have been forcibly prevented from conceiving. You are the only man who can do anything to help him. The other two clots will not have a car in their places at this time of the year. Be a sport and lend him your own. You are so busy coining money that you never have time to spend it. A good engine is made to be used. Nothing spoils a good car more than leaving it idle while you count the money in your till.'

'Well — ' began Voisin senior doubt-fully.

'Go on,' urged M. Pinaud's new-found friend, in no way exhausted by the eloquence of his own verbosity. 'I told you he was a good type. He will pay you the full seasonal rate and probably add a bonus if you oblige him. There is no mistaking a generous type. Besides, a driver of his calibre deserves a quality car — something rather larger and faster than a baby Citroën.'

Voisin senior looked at him thoughtfully for a long moment. Then he replied quietly.

'You have a good point there, my friend. I will go and check it.'

And he walked away to the back of the shed. M. Pinaud too looked very thoughtfully at the bus-driver.

'Look, m'sieu,' he said. 'Before we begin to exchange names and addresses for the insurance companies — tell me why you are doing this to help me — you do not even know me — '

The man held up his hand with an entirely unconscious and therefore all the more impressive authority and dignity. His eyes, stern and inflexible and yet at the same time warm and compassionate — the eyes of a soldier — looked straight into his own as he answered without the slightest hesitation.

'Because — without knowing you, m'sieu, or even caring one brass *centime* who you are — I am proud and privileged, as I told you, to have shaken your hand. All my life I have commanded men. I have sent them to their death. And I know a man when I see one.'

* * *

Voisin senior came to them from the back of the shed.

'Would you come with me, M'sieu Pinaud?' he asked, and walked away without waiting for an answer.

M. Pinaud's eyes glistened as he saw the car behind the outer door. It was an enormous vintage Panhard-Levassor in immaculate show-room condition. Model *grande tourisme*. A car in a thousand. He opened his mouth to speak but the quiet voice forestalled him.

'You have a good champion, M'sieu Pinaud. You heard what he said about you. I would not have listened to anyone else, but he is a man I respect.'

'Who is he?' asked M. Pinaud curiously. 'He has just given me particulars of the bus company. Surely he is an unusual type for a bus-driver?'

The garage owner smiled.

'He was once the celebrated Colonel Aigremont. He spent two years in Fresnes military prison during the war for refusing to obey a general's command to lead his regiment into a death-trap in the Ardennes. The surrender saved him from being shot.'

M. Pinaud smiled as well.

'That explains a good deal,' he said. 'I share your feelings, M'sieu Voisin, and believe me I am most grateful for your help.'

'It is a pleasure. I would do anything for that man. A few more like him and there might have been no Vichy — no surrender. Now give me an hour to check my car once again and fill the tank. Go and have a drink and then when you come back I will show you how everything works and you can drive it away.'

'Thank you very much.'

★　★　★

233

He walked to the nearest *café*, sat outside in one of the wicker chairs and ordered a large absinthe. He had been told by his father at an early and impressionable age never to mix his drinks . . .

He needed a drink, after what had happened. He needed a large one. But after all those years he could still see as vividly as yesterday the loving face with its magnificently broad and high forehead, still hear the quiet and ironical voice and still feel the touch of that beautiful watchmaker's hand — tapering, sensitive and strong . . .

And so he remembered the good advice.

He watched the people passing on the pavement and did not see them. The wind was rising, the clouds were banking together once more. Soon it would rain again.

Now he had smashed another car. M. le Chef would be furious. He would have to be convinced that the accident had not been his own fault. He ought to telephone. M. le Chef would be waiting for news. But he would have to continue to wait.

An attentive waiter came out and in answer to his affirmative nod rushed in again.

At the moment he had other things to think about, more important thoughts to occupy his mind. What could have happened to Denise Roche? Where had the taxi taken her?

He sat there without moving, suffering under the torment of his vivid imagination, until gradually his sight seemed to clear and he saw the moving people once again.

Outstanding in his black suit amidst the gaily assorted and colourful patterns of all the holiday clothes, he saw the figure of a priest passing along the pavement. The narrow white collar and black vest triggered off a sudden spate of memories, but they were all confused even as they flooded his mind. But somehow he knew that they were important, and so he concentrated on them long after the priest had gone.

It was at school. It had been at school. His history master had been a priest. He did not have to close his eyes. He could see him now clearly in his mind. He had worn a similar black suit and collar, with a plain gold cross suspended from a gold chain around his neck. But that had been a long time ago.

The waiter was rewarded for his devoted attention with another nod. It was a pity, M. Pinaud reflected, that he had not paid more attention to this master's history lessons. He had never been very interested in history. The people were now dead, he had considered with the arrogance of youth, so what could it all really matter? But in spite of his dogmatic opinion he had been fascinated by the way this born instructor had been capable — only by reading in his dominant, convincing and erudite preaching voice some of the notes he had made himself for his university scholarship — capable of making people — who had been such bastards that they were surely far better dead — making them live once again so vividly that one young boy in the front of the class could actually see them in their robes or in their armour on the scarred wooden front of that massive raised desk . . .

He emptied his glass, got up from the chair and walked back to the garage.

He listened while Voisin senior explained the controls with a befitting respect. Then he drove the magnificent car very slowly out of the garage with a fully justified emotion compounded of awe, respect and exultation. On this one there was nothing so common, trite or banal as moving a lever to engage a gear, as he had done so many times on all the cars he had driven. The action was more like cutting butter with a very sharp knife.

12

He had listened to Voisin senior with only part of his mind. The other subconscious part had been working all the time in its own incredible way.

Now as he drove down the promenade the confusion suddenly became clear and he remembered. He remembered the master again. And he remembered that particular history lesson. He remembered, suddenly and with a vivid clarity, that it had been about the Huguenot persecutions in the reign of Louis XIV, and how it was a fully authenticated historical fact that there had been hiding-places actually built into the houses and cottages that were under construction at the time, since there had been no lack of evidence and proof that these persecutions were bound to continue and increase.

He saw it all as if in the blinding light of a revelation. He had searched

Madoule's cottage, but he had failed, because at that time he had no idea of what it was that he had been trying to find.

Now he knew. Now he remembered the thickness of the walls. He knew that he was right.

He pressed the accelerator and the car surged forward in a burst of impressive speed. This was a masterpiece of engineering. This was a car made with the weight and the solidity of a tank and activated by a power-unit that reminded him of a railway-engine. He roared up the road to the headland in a great burst of speed, put the car in neutral gear, switched off the engine and coasted silently along until he was outside the fisherman's cottage.

He got out without a sound, left the door open and walked noiselessly to the door of the cottage.

The light was on in the kitchen. He drew his gun from its shoulder-holster, grasped the latch and suddenly flung the door wide open.

Madoule started up from the table, a

thin-bladed kitchen-knife in his outstretched hand positioned for the deadly forward thrust.

Without hesitation he swerved, aimed and fired from an angle at the top of the man's hand. Then he slid his own along the gun until he was gripping the barrel, leapt forward and hit him just hard enough on the head with the butt.

He left him unconscious on the floor while he took a cloth from beside the sink and bound the grazed knuckles tightly to stop the bleeding. He found the knife on the floor, the handle scored by the bullet but the narrow blade still intact. Then he took the handcuffs from his hip-pocket, pulled the unconscious figure of the gypsy towards the fireplace and handcuffed both his wrists securely around the iron bars of the grate.

Then he went looking for the hiding-place. It did not take him long to find it — a small rectangular cavity in the thickness of the wall beside the massive stone fireplace. The air-ducts were skilfully concealed behind an over-lapping plank level with the upper floor. The opening was narrow and practically invisible because of the skill with which the matching flints of the wall had been plastered into place, the keyhole behind a loose one that lifted out. He found the key in a bunch on the unconscious man's belt.

Denise Roche was huddled on blankets and cushions in a space not much larger than a cupboard, but her smile was as welcome and as charming as he remembered it.

'Are you all right?' he asked.

'Yes — I knew you would come.'

'Then you knew more than I did,' he told her. 'Look — ' he went on quickly, 'are you sure you are quite all right — they did not hurt you?'

'No — no — why do you ask?'

'Because I would like you to stay here for a little longer. Do you mind?'

'No — of course not. Not if you want me to. But why?'

'I have one of them here, handcuffed and unconscious. But I am sure one or two more will be coming to this place very shortly. I want to get them all and finish this thing for good. Will you be all right?'

'Yes. I told you. I have not been here for long. Do what you have to do.'

'Thank you, Denise. I shall be here in the next room. Bang on the panel if you want me. Then I shall be outside, waiting for them to come. The panel is unlocked — here is a clasp-knife. Use it on the latch and look after yourself if something goes wrong.'

⋆　⋆　⋆

He left her and went to the kitchen. There he filled a bowl with cold water from the tap, took it back to the fireplace and threw the water over Madoule's head.

The gypsy stirred with the shock and moaned, moving his head slowly from side to side.

M. Pinaud knelt down beside him, one hand at his throat, forcing his head back against the raised bricks into which the fire-bars were set, the other holding the knife point against his cheek, just below one eye.

The brown eyes opened wide with an agonised terror that was more than fear. M. Pinaud's above them were cold and implacable, his voice hard and merciless.

'They will be coming here to-night — someone will come to see that she is safely here.'

This gypsy had been useful with his cottage but his had not been the master-mind that had organised the whole thing. He tightened his hand on the man's throat and moved the knife. The razor-sharp point of the blade opened the skin beneath one eye and the blood trickled down his cheek, but the head, clamped in that iron grip, could not move.

'You will tell me the truth — or else your eye will be on the floor. Then the other one. You will be blind. Then I will take this knife lower down.'

His voice was frightening with an infinite menace, enough to stimulate the terrified gypsy into finding his own.

'Yes — yes — ' he gasped. 'They always come — when it is dark — to see — to check — '

M. Pinaud dropped the knife on the floor and stood up. Would he have used it, he wondered. Then he remembered the face of the dead child in the morgue and knew that he would never have hesitated, not for one second . . .

He left all the lights on in the cottage and went outside to the car. The rain had come in with the evening tide and was now pouring down steadily.

He started the engine and moved the car to conceal it behind the far wall of the cottage. Here he would be able to see anyone coming up the road and from here he could also drive out, suddenly and unexpectedly, and approach from the back.

Then he switched off the engine, extinguished the lights, lit a cigarette and settled down in the seat, prepared to wait for as long as was necessary.

At first his thoughts were confused and bitter. He tried to think of the explanations he would have to give to M. le Chef for smashing up another car. He remembered the letters he had read from the kidnapper and he thought of those parents who had been unable to find the ransom money. He thought of Mansard the jeweller and of how he must have found out something, some clue which made him a danger that had to be eliminated. He thought again of Mansard's child. He thought of his own young daughters, happy and carefree on their grandparents' farm and of what his reactions would have been if this had happened to one of them. He thought of the kidnapper, how often he had succeeded. He thought of all the money involved. He knew how lawyers, juries and even judges, in this corrupt day and age, could be influenced, biassed and even directed by its overwhelming power . . .

He lit another cigarette. There was nothing else to do, except to wait. They would come in the end. He only had to wait.

And then, suddenly, the confusion of all his thoughts seemed to align themselves, miraculously and unexpectedly, into an orderly pattern. Now he could see a motive, a design and a sequence, directed by some unseen hand. He himself had been powerless. The decisions made had not been his.

The plan had been to follow Denise Roche in the taxi. But why should the child have chosen that particular moment to run out into the road? Why should the bus-driver have happened to know the garage-owner, so that he was now — in spite of the accident — sitting at the wheel of a far larger and more powerful car than his own? Why should he have had to wait in a *café* before he could drive it, so that he had been able to see the passing priest and remember the lessons of his schoolmaster which gave him the clue to discover the hiding-place in the cottage and so find Denise Roche?

He had been told about absinthe when he was very young. But why had he ordered it from the Italian in the first place, when trying to find out some information about Marc Lebrun? Because of what he had been told he continued to drink it in the other *café* on the promenade while waiting for the Panhard to be made ready. And therefore he had been able to see the priest on the pavement and start thinking about all the things that eventually gave him the solution to the problem . . .

* * *

He sat there in the wind and the wet and the darkness of the driving rain, alone with his thoughts. There were many, and now they followed each other in a sequence of ordered logic, but always through them, in a sombre streak of sadness, ran the memories of that small dead body he had seen in the morgue. The pattern and the design were now clear — but the pain that was part of them he knew would always endure.

He had already made up his mind — characteristically without hesitation — but he did not know it. He only knew that he was prepared to wait, for as long as might be necessary, for this was why he had been sent here, and this was his duty as he saw it.

When the taxi eventually came he was already in the correct position. He started the engine, engaged the gear, switched on his headlights and shot suddenly out of concealment up the cliff track behind it.

In the glare of the powerful headlights he verified the identical registration number he had noted outside the station. This had been the first taxi which Denise Roche had taken. And in their same bright illumination he recognised Inspector Dumont as he turned in the back seat at the sudden glare.

This was a complete and unexpected surprise, but he realised at once how logically this answer fitted in with the whole pattern. This explained — in a sudden and shocking flash of understanding — why Dumont had been unable to achieve anything by his investigations, why he had always stalled and prevaricated, why he had misled him with false suspects and why he had paid Lebrun to stop him interfering.

He remembered the Inspector's remarks when he had first met him about the choice jobs in the larger departments. The temptation of the money had been too great for an ambitious and unscrupulous man relegated to this comparatively obscure backwater — great enough to lead him to betray his oath and his position of trust and to bring agony and torment to innocent people.

He thought how a really first-class lawyer, who could command an exorbitant fee because of his encyclopaedic knowledge of the law, could easily make a mockery of any official charges against Dumont. As the man himself had said, there was no proof and there was no evidence.

Dumont could claim that because of his reasonable suspicions he had ordered the taxi-driver to take him to the cottage of Madoule, whom he had long suspected. Who could prove otherwise? The taxi-driver would be imprisoned — and quite possibly might be found dead in his cell in the morning. One of the prison warders might be suspected — the average pay is not high — or the capsule might have been successfully enough hidden to escape a search. Madoule the gypsy would never tell the truth. It was not in his nature. He would swear whatever he was paid to say.

Legally, there must be proof and there must be evidence.

He did not hesitate.

He sent the powerful car roaring up behind the taxi and in a final burst of savage and irresistible speed crashed it into its rear bumpers.

The driver jammed on his brakes, but the wheels locked and skidded on the wet surface of the track and the grass verge, and the power and the momentum of the Panhard's great engine sent the taxi, completely out of control, to smash through the wooden fence and over the edge of the cliff down into the sea below.

The chassis hit a projecing ledge of rock and the petrol tank exploded into flames which the dark surging waters quickly extinguished.

And then there was nothing as he swung the car inland, applied the brakes and switched off the engine — nothing at all. Only the wind and the rain and the darkness all around him and the wild savage tumult of his thoughts . . .

For a moment he felt the remorse and compunction of that sorrow which never failed to accompany the emotion in his cases, either as a sudden stab or a slow silent stealing, a sorrow that would stay with him, softly and sadly, long after the case was closed. He was a humane man and a compassionate one; in his work these qualities were tested to the utmost limit of endurance. It is to his credit that he emerged from the ordeal his work made of his life with these qualities untouched, unaffected and unchanged. If anything, they were strengthened and intensified by all the violence and misery and horror he was compelled to witness and endure.

But this was something different. This was an iniquity that was unspeakable, a vileness that had resulted in the small dead body he had seen in the morgue. This was a desecration that he knew might well go unpunished. This was something he felt with an utter conviction that he had been compelled to do, whatever the pain, whatever the remorse, whatever the consequences. All these weighed no more than feathers against the lead on the other side of the scales.

For a moment he felt compassion and pity. Two men's lives, however unworthy, however misused, had ended — and all the cold tragic finality of that irrevocable ending seemed suddenly to surge up and overwhelm him, since he had been the cause of that ending. For a moment he bowed his head, alone there in the quiet solemnity of the night, and prayed reverently for forgiveness and absolution.

This was the worst part. This was the part that he hated. This was the part that always made his spectacular achievements seem like child's play, his triumphs a mockery and his success a folly.

But this had been necessary. He knew that he had been right. This had been his decision, and without question he had made it.

★　★　★

He got out of the car awkwardly, stiff with cramp and weak with nervous reaction. Then he walked slowly and heavily towards the lighted cottage.

Madoule was still handcuffed to the firebars. He passed him without even looking. The ancient iron of the one and the modern steel of the other had both been made to withstand a far greater strength than the gypsy possessed.

His mind was fully occupied with a very different speculation. He was thinking of Denise Roche. He now remembered her features, her hair and her body — vividly, meticulously and excitingly. All these were not things any man could easily forget.

He felt what he would have preferred to describe — with an innate dignity bred of the mellowing influence of years of experience — as a surge of a perfectly normal if somewhat excited desire, while realising only too well that his faithful chronicler, with the insensate fervour of an enthusiastic author, was bound to type out as a mad and swelling lust . . .

But there was not very much that he could do about it, he reflected philosophically. After all, it was his chronicler who wrote and typed out all his books with two fingers and then even went out and sold them to the publishers and earnt him money.

The point at issue was a quite different and far more important one than a pedantic choice of words. He was about to rescue this very lovely girl, who had been kidnapped and locked up in a small hiding-place, as he had promised he would.

She would be grateful. She was bound to feel grateful. For an exhilarating moment he gave free rein to his vivid imagination and had not the slightest difficulty in picturing many of the interesting ways in which a young and attractive girl could show, demonstrate and prove a sincere and heartfelt gratitude . . .

He already had a room booked at the Golden Lion. There would be no practical hindrances to the implementing of her gratitude.

This was normal and logical thinking, he told himself. And even as he thought, he knew that he was no longer capable of normal thinking.

In his mind he could see — not Deputy Officer Denise Roche with all her physical allure and attraction, however much he wanted to think about her and about that — but something quite different. He could see only a small dead body, with a face that had once been alert and alive and eager. And now was still and small. And sad and dead . . .

★   ★   ★

He sighed and went to open the panel of the hiding-place.

'Come,' he said quietly, and his voice was gentle with an infinite kindness. 'This case is finished. I will take you back to Paris.'

Even as he spoke he knew that something — some power greater than himself — had put the right words into his mouth. He had sinned enough already, surely — but mercifully he had

255

been prevented from sinning even more . . .

For him now the only important thing to do was to drive back home quickly so that he could get up early in the morning and see the priest to make his confession and pray once again for absolution and forgiveness.

THE END

We do hope that you have enjoyed reading this large print book.

Did you know that all of our titles are available for purchase?

We publish a wide range of high quality large print books including:
Romances, Mysteries, Classics General Fiction Non Fiction and Westerns

Special interest titles available in large print are:
The Little Oxford Dictionary Music Book, Song Book Hymn Book, Service Book

Also available from us courtesy of Oxford University Press:
Young Readers' Dictionary (large print edition) Young Readers' Thesaurus (large print edition)

For further information or a free brochure, please contact us at:
**Ulverscroft Large Print Books Ltd., The Green, Bradgate Road, Anstey, Leicester, LE7 7FU, England.
Tel:** (00 44) **0116 236 4325
Fax:** (00 44) **0116 234 0205**

Other titles in the
Linford Mystery Library:

DEATH CALLED AT NIGHT

R. A. Bennett

Jimmy Ellis believes his parents have died in a car crash when as a young boy he is taken to live with relatives in Australia. The years pass happily, then the nightmare comes. Terrifying images flit through his mind in the dark — all through the eyes of a child, a witness to grisly events seventeen years before. He begins to delve into the past, and soon he finds himself on the trail of a double murderer — a murderer who is prepared to kill again.

THE DEAD TALE-TELLERS

John Newton Chance

Jonathan Blake always kept appointments. He had kept many, in all sorts of places, at all sorts of times, but never one like that one he kept in the house in the woods in the fading light of an October day. It seemed a perfect, peaceful place to visit and perhaps take tea and muffins round the fire. But at this appointment his footsteps dragged, for he knew that inside the house the men with whom he had that date were already dead . . .

THE CALIGARI COMPLEX

Basil Copper

Mike Faraday, the laconic L.A. private investigator, is called in when macabre happenings threaten the Martin-Hannaway Corporation. Fires, accidents and sudden death are involved; one of the partners, James Hannaway, inexplicably fell off a monster crane. Mike is soon entangled in a web of murder, treachery and deceit and through it all a sinister figure flits; something out of a nightmare. Who is hiding beneath the mask of Cesare, the somnambulist? Mike has a tough time finding out.

MIX ME A MURDER

Leo Grex

A drugged girl, a crook with a secret, a doctor with a dubious past, and murder during a shooting affray — described as a 'duel' by the Press — become part of a developing mystery in which a concealed denouement is unravelled only when the last danger threatens. Even then, the drama becomes a race against time and death when Detective Chief Superintendent Gary Bull insists on playing his key role of hostage to danger.

DEAD END IN MAYFAIR

Leonard Gribble

In another Yard case for Commander Anthony Slade, there is blackmail at London's latest night spot. Ruth Graham, a journalist, and Stephen Blaine, a blackmail victim, pit their wits against unusual odds when sudden violence erupts. Then Slade has to direct the 'Met' in a gruelling bout of police work, which involves a drugs gang and a titled mastermind who has developed blackmail into a lucrative practice. The climax to the case is both startling and brutal.